I Think I'll Stay Here Forever

I THINK I'LL STAY HERE FOREVER

GEORGE CHOUNDAS

winner of the Press 53 Award for Short Fiction

Press 53
—◆—
Winston-Salem

Press 53, LLC
PO Box 30314
Winston-Salem, NC 27130

First Edition

Cover design by Claire V. Foxx

Library of Congress Control Number
2025937544

ISBN 978-1-950413-98-0

To the Rev. George S. Burchill, who always told me to keep going.

And to Bill Kane, who showed me how.

CONTENTS

KATINGO CARRIED 15,980 TONS AND A GENTLEMAN

He was six or seven when he swam in sea that came up to his lips. It was a pocket cut off by rocks. All the boys swam there. But none were around. He felt like God. The ocean was desperate to kiss him. The world hung from his mouth.

He was swimming for urchin. *Achinous*. Like an oyster, but sweeter and gamier. An oyster that has drunk buttermilk, then gotten a little sick.

Instead he found an octopus. The thing he saw was its *katsoula*, the main body like a quivering heart. The arms he didn't see. Then one grasped his wrist. He might have pulled away. But he submerged. Youth chooses something over nothing.

With other arms it locked onto a rock at the sea bottom. A rock that *was* the sea bottom. Around and under the pointed end of an outcrop. He pulled away. The cinch on his wrist only tightened. Now his lungs were burning. He'd been underwater a good half a minute. He pulled harder. His lungs were burning.

He didn't think before doing it. In one hinging motion he ducked down and bit the octopus in the eye and clenched. It startled, released, darted away. It managed several inches before it stopped and drifted, bent over a little. Like it was trying to remember something.

The octopus wasn't heavy over his shoulder. The *katsoula* rolled back and forth across his back. It stopped smelling like waves before he got home.

The taste was still in his mouth from the eye. This, even further removed from ocean. Sere and brineless. High up. Careless of small things and busy things. He'd never been to the mountains. But it is possible to know things without having reason to know them, and he knew the taste was mountain air.

Now he is sixty. This is old for a farmer, a grocer. For a merchant seaman, who moves even when standing still, who is softer than everything around him, it is ancient. He has served on thirty-seven ships before *Katingo*. He remembers the names of all thirty-seven, their tonnage, their cargo. He remembers thirty-seven pairs of ports: where he first came aboard, where he last disembarked. Matronyms and patronyms.

He remembers things about his crewmates he didn't know he remembered. Once, wearing a face mask while chipping rust, he smelled the breath of a boatswain he'd worked for two decades earlier—pears and milk gone slightly sour, unmistakable—and turned so quickly the *matsakoni* he was holding left a dent in the bulkhead. Nobody there. The boatswain had been dead for decades. The breath he was smelling was his own.

He was boatswain himself once, on a ship so small it was rated strictly for coastal routes. It went as far as London and lost an anchor in Beaufort-7 seas. Otherwise he has served as an able-bodied. He is an able-bodied on the tanker *Katingo*, with its fat keel that laughs at Beaufort 7.

He is oldest of the crew by nearly three decades. He is older even than the Kontropontis brothers, who own the ship. This discrepancy for Greeks is awkward, even untoward. Like fourth marriages. Or holding hands at a funeral.

Nobody needs thirty-seven ships to know a new crew's first night aboard a vessel is singular. Quiet, first of all. The men are cowed, bent by novelty and strangeness to an earnest frame of mind. They have not yet grouped off. Ignorance nurtures acceptance. They still have, or will affect, a desire to learn something.

Katingo's crew, however, is not new. Only three are new, having joined at Genoa: captain, first officer, the Gentleman himself. The rest of them have been sailing together for months. The Gentleman forgets this. Somehow he has in mind this is a fresh venture for all of them. Maybe this is not an error. Maybe this is the very long view. If anything can happen, it can happen again.

A few crew gather round: Stamati, Spiro, Ianni, Tasso. A couple more from the twelve-to-four. The Gentleman is saying something about molasses ships. No one recalls how or why he arrived at the subject. They listen anyway.

There was the *Vestalasket*, a Swedish freighter. It ran from Itajaí to Brest. Carried molasses. Molasses must be kept warm in the ship's hold. Through *Vestalasket*'s cargo seethed enormous heating coils, glowing and gurgling at the bottom of that brown, deaf ocean. The heating method was customary. Not customary was the weather in that equatorial swath of the Atlantic across which *Vestalasket* made its way. Autumn, but it stayed unseasonably warm that year. Air temperatures rose so high that shippering experts still debate whether the even higher temperatures in the ship's hold may have obviated entirely the need for heating coils. In any event, this ship was wreathed in an unconscionable smell. Warm molasses, sure, but sweeter, darker, more keening, more trenchant: more. It penetrated every part of the ship. It was a heady thing, this scent, not so much for the way it smelled as for the way it made the smeller *feel*. It was a scent of pure urge. Imperious, nearly intolerable. Whoever smelled it wanted something—badly—but did not know what it was. The closest feeling was lust, but this urge had nothing to do with the loins and their rind-deep tantrums. It plumbed deeper and knifed higher, a hot anxious hole in the chest, and the tender rim of that hole prickled and throbbed with the overlivened sensation of inflamed throat and summer toothache and funny bone rung fresh against doorjamb, and with every breath of deep dark sugar, the hole would pucker and ache and very badly *want*. That wonder air unhinged the *Vestalasket*'s seamen, mad to offer their lives for whatever might sate the hot holes inside them, flummoxed about what that might be.

The ship's motion only put flame to the fever. Molasses is a peculiar cargo, liquid enough to shift constantly in search of level but viscous enough to shift slowly and stubbornly. It is an intransigent sludge that traps and intensifies whatever momentum it is afforded. For this reason the movements of a molasses ship are different from those of every other ocean-going vessel. Any given movement proceeds more gradually, yet more extremely. The feel of a molasses ship, in sum, is the feel of a dream.

Nobody who has not worked a molasses ship can understand. Odysseus, who tied himself to the mast so he could hear the siren song, who sensed first a lip-gentle summoning, a tease across the skin, spreading so innocently it could not be denied, anointing every bit of him with garden light, enrobing his cock in a velvet that furled and tugged, warmer, steadily warmer, glorious, almost perfect almost perfect and, finally, replacing his insides with a lake of sweet pain for all the things he could never have again, who understood that not yielding was the same as a thousand razors, could understand. Nobody else who has not worked a molasses ship can understand.

Combine in your mind, please, the unremitting pulse of urge and the distended feel of dream and a mounting desperation at how to reconcile these, let alone resolve them, and a panic that there can be no relief because the ship itself, the only planet under a seaman's feet, is

responsible, and you'll understand how men without
religion will pray absurd and impossible prayers, not for
a safe and speedy journey to port, but for the ship to be
there, now, already there, immediately there, there *now*.

"When were you on a molasses ship?" Stamati asks
the Gentleman.

"You're the lawyer," says the Gentleman, so matter-
of-factly he may be talking to himself. "Every crew has
a lawyer."

Stamati wears two pairs of shorts to sleep. The pay he
sends home is all his parents and sisters have. Wearing
two shorts lets him ignore the blood that seeps out by
morning. Were the Gentleman to get to know Stamati,
he'd know Stamati is no lawyer. But the Gentleman will
never get to know Stamati. The Gentleman continues.
Neither Stamati nor anyone else thinks to stop him.

This Swedish freighter had a clever chief officer. He
hit upon a way to focus his unsettled crew and vent their
wildness: safety drills. Fire, collision, man overboard,
abandon ship.

Eighteen drills in five days. Eighteen drills, and then
the drills were suspended.

Because during the nineteenth drill aboard *Fourth
Star*, one of the crew—

"I thought the ship was *Vestalasket*," Stamati
interrupts. Not a little haughtily. Like a lawyer, really.

The Gentleman pauses, then resumes, without change
in tone or pace. Wave against rock.

During the nineteenth drill aboard *Vestalasket*,
someone noticed the missing deckhand. The third officer
went to find him. Minutes later, then many minutes later:
still no news from the deckhand, and now the third officer
was disappeared. It was the steward who, passing by the
captain's cabin, saw the door to the cabin swinging freely
and, inside, spied both missing men. On the bed was the
captain, on hands and knees, naked. Standing behind
him was the deckhand, wearing only pants and shoes and
making love to the captain's backside. Standing in front

of the captain, but facing away, was the third officer. He was bent over. He rested his forearms on his own thighs, and wore only a shirt, and this shirt was flung up over the back of his bent frame and his neck and part of his head too. The captain, face buried in the third officer's ass, was sobbing.

Shirt and pants and the nakedness underneath: the three wore the costume of a single man.

Standing and bending and kneeling: the postures of a single man.

Avid, resolute, miserable. His varying heart.

Then there was an American ship that carried molasses from Mobile to Newark.

"You don't have stories about Greek ships?" Tasso interjects, laughing with his whole laundry-bag abdomen.

"You like stories about what you already know?" The Gentleman makes a sound in his throat, as if to clear away the foulness of this inanity. "Everybody raise their hand, they want to hear this man tell a story about shitting and farting. Nobody? What a surprise. What a shock."

Tasso looks around, still laughing. He is too comfortable for humiliation.

The Gentleman never tells stories about himself. The youngsters need to learn ships, to hear about ships. He doesn't tell them about the roofless jail in Curaçao, the inmate he saw there, hair to his elbows, face half gone from cancer, who maintained very steadily, if you asked him, that he'd been there thirty years.

Or about Osaka, where they sent him to take a wiper and an ordinary to see a doctor. Both had burned with fever for over a week. Normally the second officer would administer a trip like that. But others on the crew had started fevers two days previously, and the officers, scared of contagion, didn't want to go ashore. It made no sense. If there was contagion, it was aboard the vessel, not in Osaka. But the Gentleman had some

Japanese from years ago, when he'd spent three months on a refurbish crew at Yokohama. Now they gave him both patients and too much cash and the Osaka agent's phone number and six hours.

They spent most of that time waiting for the doctor. No reception room. Instead they were shown into a tiny outdoor courtyard by a young woman, prim and impassive and sharp-boned, wearing a white pleated skirt. The courtyard was pleasant, in fact. There were flowers everywhere like little sunburned cheeks. It was only after they seated themselves in wicker chairs, when she offered the men a last settling look before returning to the clinic proper, that the Gentleman realized with a start she was only a girl, nine, maybe eight.

By the time they finished at the clinic and took a car to the port, it was dark, and they were half an hour late. Unbelievably, the ship had left without them. The Gentleman would learn later that the captain himself had come down with fever and suffered in his cabin, and the first officer, wishing not to appear weak, had overcompensated.

Freshly abandoned, the Gentleman knew none of this. The three men went to the lobby of a posh hotel where the Gentleman used the telephone. He called and called and made a point of doing this with exquisite calm. Neither of his shipmates suspected his fury.

The Osaka agent wasn't picking up. The Osaka agent had gone home.

"Let's stay the night," the ordinary joked, surveying the lobby's ceiling.

"No," the Gentleman said. "It wouldn't be right."

They left, and the Gentleman brought them in taxi to a different, still more luxurious hotel. It had glass doors that, from the street, revealed only a kind of heaven-puzzle: honeycombing light, bright shining angles. As they crossed the lobby it was the wiper who observed that the pile underfoot was half again as thick as the last hotel's carpet.

One room for one night cost the rest of the cash. The Gentleman slept on the floor. Neither the wiper nor the ordinary had ever slept in a hotel. Neither spoke as they got carefully in bed, not even to pretend it didn't mean so much.

"Shut up, Tasso," Spiro says.

Spiro steals from Ianni, who bunks in the next cabin. Spiro doesn't want anything from Ianni. He wants, more or less, to *be* Ianni. Or at least to imagine he is, and a comb helps, and a handkerchief.

"Just—let him talk" is what Ianni would say, which is why Spiro says it. Even though Ianni is right there and not saying it.

Tasso snorts. "I'm not stopping anybody from anything."

When the rasp of the Gentleman's fingers against his own cheek is the only sound, he continues.

Two engineers fell into an argument. One of them got hold of a flare gun. He shot the other in the chest. The flare knocked the man over and caromed out over a deck rail. The flare stopped the man's heart. When after a minute the man stirred—his heart started up again— he coughed. Out of his mouth plumed the same dense gray smoke that pours from a lit flare.

On another American molasses ship—Americans have the most stories, America is a story, and ants in a dunghill like to make more dung—the chief officer himself climbed onto the stern rail. As if to leave no doubt that this was not impulse but a considered venture, he perched for a frozen moment on the rail, pressed his hands together over his head like a showboating child, and dove an arc into following waters. For three hours he treaded. He ignored his friends' entreaties to swim closer. He disregarded his superiors' increasingly shrill demands to take hold of each successive rescue device thrown to him. Finally he was retrieved. Asked why for three hours he had appeared to work his hardest not to allow himself rescue, he pointed out that safe operation was the chief mate's responsibility and explained: if he threw himself overboard, with all the shouting and excitement and logistics, nobody else would.

Once, a molasses ship docked in evening at Milazzo and could not be unloaded by approved stevedores until two the next afternoon. That night it brought a whole suburb of smell to the port town, a scent of dark intimacy, of treats iced with risk. The air swelled and spread its swirling precipitate of mights and coulds. The smell tendriled out to the water-facing street and the foothill street behind it. Not once but twice, men from the town tried to get aboard the ship. They were repelled both times, but the second time the men on port watch, addled, nearly beat the intruders to death without especially meaning to.

Men on shore leave from molasses ships report anomalies. They get frank and disproportionate looks. These are not the standard communications of interest: animal slyness, head cants, smiles. These are startled looks, looks of wonder, the kind two people indoors who hear a detonation outdoors give each other to ask, What is happening? Is something happening? In bed the men have the molasses odor sunk into their skin, and their lovers beat it out of them with their crotches and pry it out of them with their tongues and try to snatch it out of them with their ten fingers and two nipples and ten toes. They put these flesh parts to prodding and gouging. They are needy like cobra charmers in front of a supper crowd to finally raise a teat of some kind from that stubborn skin, so that they might, must, now, suckle out the rich brown candy broth so obviously on offer.

They want to hear about storms. Everybody wants to hear about storms. Let them learn about ships first. Walk before running. Youth thinks it knows things it doesn't know, and this is the same as peril. They know with waves at ten feet the steward wets the tablecloths, and at twenty feet the bow watch wears a harness.

They don't know that time in the North Atlantic, winter, when the waves reached thirty feet and nobody could see them. The sky had turned so black it sucked the shine out of the ship's lights. The lamps seemed bits of paint. The wind sheared at the ship, made whistles from its parts, made from these a keening whole. The ship, in short, was screaming.

It was just as the rain started—in great lashing sheets—that the Gentleman saw Dimitri, the ordinary from the eight-to-twelve watch, barely twenty years old, lift off the deck of the ship on a gust of wind, blow over the port rail, and vault into the black.

This is not why the Gentleman remembers. He remembers because of what happened next. After a good half a minute, he heard a scrambling thud on the deck. Like a sack dropped and come undone. It was Dimitri. The storm had spat him and his boy limbs back onto the ship—*but from over the opposite rail.* Two other men saw this.

An hour later Dimitri woke up. He didn't eat much and said nothing, no matter what they asked him. When finally he did speak, he said only one word: *When?* Those who heard it understood it was a question, despite the flat tone.

A day later he was eating well enough that the officers decided he didn't need a hospital. Still he said only a single word, in greeting, in response, his only sound: *When?*

Three days later, the captain altered course for the nearest port. Physically Dimitri was the picture of health. But he had them worried, still saying just the one word.

Nobody ever learned if or when Dimitri got out of the hospital, got better, whether he ever returned to the ships or went home to Aegina. It was all speculation. That he was convinced even after tumbling out of the storm, even as he convalesced, that he would soon die, and this is why he asked, *When?* That he was ripped out of the intelligible world so viciously, and shoved back so abruptly, that he entirely missed the second part, the part where he returned, and this is why he asked, *When?* That a man who, to all appearances, had flown around the world in one piece would know very well, better than the ancients among us and the most profound, that anything was possible, that all was inevitable, that everything that could be fathomed was destined to happen, it was only a matter of time, and so he asked the only question that mattered: *When?*

Instead the Gentleman says: There are three kinds of ships to which Greek captains give wide berth.

First, dry cargo ships carrying explosive materials or bomb parts. Each of these is a stuck valve away from disaster. None sane loves to share close ocean with them.

Second, Norwegian ships in winter. They carry two cargoes: the stuff in their holds and inebriates. The man at the helm, like as not, will be drunk and unaccountable. His motivations, obscure and fluctuating. There is every reason to steer generously around.

"That's not true," Ianni says.

"Just shut up," Petro says. Petro hates himself and the sound of his own voice. Ianni knows Petro talks only when he is upset.

"He doesn't know what he's talking about," Ianni says, without rancor.

"You're a famous idiot," Petro says.

"Most of the sailors on Norwegian ships aren't even Norwegian."

"What?"

"A quarter of them are Spaniards. From Spain."

"I know where Spaniards come from."

"Most of the rest are Danish and British. Not too many Norwegians on Norwegian ships. Everybody knows."

"You're proving his point."

"What?"

"That's his point. They have to constantly replace the Norwegians. They're always falling overboard. They're drunk, they're wandering into the ocean. Of course they need Spaniards. Just shut up and listen."

Third, molasses ships in summer. Molasses ships in summer are like Norwegian ships in winter. Except drunks are unaccountable in accountable ways, while sugar-mad sailors are unaccountable in unaccountable ways. A Norwegian helmsman in winter will steer straight for a passing vessel. He will overlook the need to do otherwise. A sugar-mad helmsman in summer will steer straight for a passing vessel. He will think it carries his darling.

The Gentleman stops and looks in the faces of the seamen around him. "Don't you see?" he says, with such vigor that it gives him a coughing fit. He goes red in the face, then pales again. "Don't you see?"

"See what?" ask Ianni and Spiro, almost at the same time.

"See what?" asks Stamati, like a third knife.

"Even the lawyer is not so smart," says the Gentleman. Stamati looks exasperated. He never purported to be a lawyer.

"An oil tanker is almost the same as a molasses ship. The cargo is liquid but thick." The Gentleman says this with his eyes closed, nodding. "If the ship moves a little, then the ship moves a lot. And the smell? Well, you know, lawyer. You've been on tankers before. The smell is from between the earth's legs. Deep musk. You don't want to smell it and you want to smell it."

The men bend closer. They want to know. They already know. From above they look like a fist closing around a gray wool scrap.

"It's a vapor that catches in your heart. Breathe too much of it and finally you're sure. You don't want to live the next day like the last fifty. You don't want to be anything forever. The world is too big. You want the chance at everything. The lawyer understands."

Stamati does not look like he understands.

"Only the possibility is real, that's what's real," the Gentleman says, then opens his mouth still wider, with no sound, as if on the brink of pronouncement, but all that comes out is a stuck winch noise. He's just clearing his throat. He pauses to taste and continues. "It's the possibility we want."

It was Babi, the four-to-eight ordinary, who found him the next morning. The Gentleman had fallen out of bed. No blood or bruise. Just age. He was grasping his bedclothes with both hands. The sheet and wool blanket had slid out of the bed with him. It looked less like he'd fallen out than like he was climbing determinedly back in. As witness, Babi had to do paperwork, along with the chief officer, and so was spared further business with the body.

An hour later, it was Tasso who changed the Gentleman's shoes. He put on the old man's best shoes, which were his other pair. He did this with exquisite calm, so nobody could suspect his grief. He didn't do this to make it easier for Ianni and Spiro to wrap the body in plastic sheeting and place it in the walk-in cooler, but he knew it would. Neither spoke as they walked it carefully to the far end, not even to pretend they weren't surprised at how heavy it carried.

A day later, they had a ceremony. There'd be one in the mountain town in Epirus where the Gentleman's only surviving relative lived, a cousin, after the body was returned. But this was the ship's memorial. The captain was probably the most religious among them, and he didn't believe in God. They sang the national anthem. When it was time for anyone to say anything, Petro knew nobody wanted to say small busy things just to say them. But he knew what they all were thinking. The silence didn't get any less impatient, and finally he jutted out his chin and said it: "None of us want to die forgotten. We won't forget him." Someone cleared his throat, and mistaking the sound for confusion, Petro tried to clarify. "We can't forget each other."

Three days later, they went running to the second officer.

"The old man," one of them choked, out of breath. They explained, taking turns, blurting over each other, not making sense. Finally Stamati took over and disciplined the message. The body was missing. The body with its plastic sheeting was gone from the cooler. Nobody awake had seen anything. The cook who discovered the blank space in the cooler could not stop crossing himself.

The second officer knew, without having reason to know, there would be nothing to find. But he said it anyway, a single word, a question.

THE WONDER OF LIGHT RAIL

The train conductor makes his way down the aisle. He's collecting tickets. He asks for yours. You give it to him. He continues down the aisle.

Ten minutes later, you hear behind you, "Tickets, tickets." It's the conductor again, making his way down the aisle. He's moving in the same direction as before, forward through the train. This means he must have passed you and returned to the rear of the train and doubled back. But you never saw him pass. This time, he's not asking everyone for their tickets—only particular passengers, presumably those who've just boarded.

But he stops at your seat and asks for your ticket. You tell him you already gave him your ticket. He says, "Be that as it may, I still need a ticket." You suspect he does not know what "be that as it may" means. You say again that you've already given it to him and that you received no receipt. He moves on but with his face in a squinch, suggesting he's dissatisfied with this state of affairs and plans to right it.

Twenty minutes later, again without you seeing him walk back down the aisle, he approaches from behind and asks for your ticket, in a way that suggests he's never seen you before in his life. You tell him that nothing's changed, that you've given him your ticket.

"Look," he says, "I don't want a speech, just a ticket."

He says this and does not wait to finish before moving on, which suggests to you he will be back. As you wait, you think about how "tickets" said over and over sounds like "stick it."

Thirty minutes later, he is back. From the same direction as always and asking for a ticket. You say you've already given him a ticket.

He says, "Why don't I remember that?"

You say, "I don't know. We've talked about this twice before. Do you remember *that*?"

And he says, "I don't like games. I'm a conductor. I'm not here for games. This isn't a game. I just need a ticket." He moves on.

Sure enough, forty minutes later, here he is, asking you for a ticket. You hand him a piece of ham. He takes it and moves on.

Fifty minutes later, you hand him a pencil. He takes it and moves on.

You continue to give him things, whatever you can muster, until the train stops at your station. As you get off the train, you hear a voice behind you.

"Your luggage, sir."

You did not board with luggage, you have no luggage. The conductor hands you a traveling case and disappears into the train. You look inside the case as the train rumbles off. Inside is everything you gave the conductor—the mongongo leaves have wilted, the egret looks discouraged—plus a train ticket for a destination you've never heard of.

The next morning you decide to take this new train to see where it goes. You give a different train conductor your ticket. Twenty minutes later he comes around again and asks for a ticket. Thirty minutes later, the same thing.

You give him broken crockery, the orange reflective triangle from the back of an Amish buggy.

When forty minutes later he asks again for your ticket, you say, "I get it. This is, like, an allegory, right? The world wants what you don't have. But it'll take what you can give. A metaphor for life, right?"

The conductor looks at you like you are a penance. He says, "I need a ticket, sir. Honestly, what I'd really like is your silence. But I'll just take a ticket." You mistake this rudeness for frustration, and you wonder if it means he finally remembers you from before.

But no. He does not remember you. He is just rude, a rude grump.

You give him a handful of spelt. He seems content to take it.

You settle in for a nap. You have a good fifty minutes.

HEEDLESS OF THE WIND AND WEATHER

There are plenty of things I should have understood but didn't. How many times have I scraped my lips with these teeth for not seeing the signs, for not realizing the love of my life was loving another? I went with him to a work function, colleagues and cocktails. I prepared by showering and pasting with a leading-brand deodorant and dressing. I did not prepare by calling to mind the physical cues of treachery. At the party I was introduced to the finest project manager in the western hemisphere. I assumed only some percentage of this was true. A hemisphere is large. I noticed this project manager kept her hands at her sides—no, pointed her arms down plumb like vectors—and with each hand rubbed preciously the tip of her thumb against the first two fingers. It was the tic of a child. I've seen it in schoolyards, never in an office. It said she knew an excellent secret. It said she was getting through the day by dwelling very deliberately on the hunk of chocolate cake with chocolate buttercream that waited for her at home in the fridge. This is how this woman was rubbing her fingers together. Turns out she had a secret—I wouldn't say an excellent one—and turns out she had a piece of cake waiting, and that cake was my husband. Turns out it was a hundred percent true if you changed western to southern and said it dirty. *Mmm, whose southern hemisphere has a big project for me to manage?* We should, all of us, know that a hard slap on the back coming out of a hug is how a man says to anybody watching, Please don't think I'm having an affair with this one—because of course I'm having an affair with this one. Hummingbird fingers look like anticipatory delight but signify guilt, plain old guilty conscience venting through the ends of the limbs. I, however, didn't know this. I did not inherit the instincts for understanding any of this. After all, no amount of betrayal and heartbreak stops us from the folly of trying again, and procreating, and thus making sure the obliviousness and vulnerability pass to the next generation. Believe me, I'm the surest proof. Right up those stairs is my seven-year-old, in the bathroom making mud-bombs from this morning's coffee grounds and taking too long for imagining all the times it will turn out different now that he has his trusty mud-bombs. Right here, down at my feet, this is my three-year-old sitting hard against one ankle and hugging the other because part of her doesn't know she'll be stepped on, and part of her wants to be stepped on. It's suddenly Christmas in the foyer of my home: commotion like a chest of drawers, frigid wool off-gassing its appliance-showroom smell, and just lots of hugs. We're having the family over, and they're freshly arrived. And here I am in mid-hug, chin lapped dumbly over my mother's shoulder, seeing my second husband, the new love of my new life, as he comes out of a hug with my sister and slaps her on the back and moves on, turning his head smooth like I've never seen before, her head the opposite, her head pointing carefully away and bobbing nervously like a missile that's lost its fix. I think I'll stay here. I think I'll rest here, on my mother, my mother of eighty-six years, who can't reach her honey-brittle arms around me, who has swelled my cells with genetic legacy and bequeathed me kindness and a trusting nature, which are the same as gullibility, who can't protect me from anything anymore. I think I'll stay here forever because what else is there, watching my husband and my sister and breathing in my mother, wondering which of these has betrayed me the most.

THE SON OF BUTT TRUDD

Eric Trudd did not mean to humiliate me. He also did not mean for his breath to smell like boiled egg. And yet.

Eric and I were in kindergarten together. He lived in the apartment above his father's upholstery shop.

In first grade, he wore white jeans every day and begged people to write on them in chalk to show how invisible it would be. No one did.

In second grade, he brought a ukulele to school. Each time someone asked if he could play, he said, "I guess you'll have to find out." He never played. No one found out.

In third grade, his mother died. He was out for a week. The day he came back, Alison Derby in her pressed khaki skirt told him we'd named the trash can "Eric." She told him he'd have to go by another name.

"No one else was using the name," she told him. "You understand, don't you?"

The next day, Alison in her gold Add-a-Bead necklace told Eric that since he still hadn't picked, the class had picked for him.

"I'm sorry, Butt," she said, "but we just can't have the confusion. You understand, Butt, don't you?"

Twice my mother brought me with her to Eric's father's shop. I didn't like it. It made me sad to think Eric and his father might be embarrassed to have people know they lived in the small apartment upstairs. It made me ashamed to think I was the one assuming they would be embarrassed for people to know. Plus I imagined Eric's socks on the floor above my head.

I should be clear about something. There was a reason I was so attuned to Eric's circumstance. I had been classmates with both Eric and Alison for three-and-a-half years. For three-and-a-half years, when Alison wasn't making fun of Eric, she was making fun of me. There was nothing about me that begged to be made fun of. At least I don't think there was, looking back, although self-assessment is a tricky thing. I was quiet, maybe, and compared to most of the other girls I dressed rather plainly but not so much that I stood out. On the other hand, there was nothing especially enchanting about me, I suppose. And my main interests—sewing, baking, listening to Billy Joel while sewing or baking—were homebody pursuits that my school peers weren't in a position to appreciate.

In any event, my interest in Eric was, in fact, the abiding interest of a fellow prisoner listening at the torturer's door. And after Eric's mother passed, and the novelty of his re-christening waned, it was soon clear— even to Alison and her mineral heart—that Eric was so comprehensively pitiful there could be no further relish in abusing him.

I became her sole project.

There was the time Alison brought cupcakes to class for her birthday and handed them out and, as she put one on my desk, shoved her thumb in the frosting, disregarding me entirely and staring instead at this thumb, as if fascinated, leaving it there for a good seven, eight seconds.

There was the time Alison and I faced off in gym class during Steal the Bacon and cagily circled the ball and one another, braced and scrutinizing for the slightest advantage, whereupon Alison suddenly straightened and gave her face a ruined expression and declared in so flat and unsensational a tone that the truth of it could not be questioned, "No fair, Mr. Salvetti, Wendy farted," and held her hand to her throat as she walked the hunched, precious, incremental walk of the freshly injured to the sideline.

There was the time Alison took out a classified in the school newsletter asking for the return of a misplaced Jordache wallet and directing those with information to my name and number—and this a good while after that fashion label's peak, when association with it had become social catastrophe, and just before (in fact, kind of the reason behind) the prohibition at St. Mary's on students placing classified ads without written parental approval.

But the worst was the day Alison made me cry at lunchtime. I don't remember what she did on that particular occasion to reduce me to tears. That I was crying doesn't narrow it down.

What I do remember is what happened when we returned from lunch. I had my face in my hands. The class bell rang, and I was still crying.

Suddenly it was Eric Trudd's voice I heard. He sounded crazed. He was shouting. "Look, she has diseases!" is what he was shouting, "She has diseases!" I looked up. Eric was out of his seat, pointing at my arms. I looked at these arms. They were so filthy from lunch recess that my tears had left long, shivery streaks that snaked down nearly to the elbows. The streaks in their desperation hadn't bothered agreeing on a single route.

I saw these monstrous, murk-borne, saline-tentacled jellyfish that were my limbs, and it seems to me now, remembering back, that I might have had time only to rove my eyes back up to Eric because before I could do anything else, Eric came closer and whispered to me, as the other kids laughed and laughed:

"Don't worry. I still like you." He whispered this.

Most of the human body is dumb meat. Generally speaking we are soft equipment. Only the core portion is alive—that warm throbbing column that extends from the center of the skull to the pit of the gut, where the detritus trapped by our plastic exteriors is processed into thought and distilled into feeling.

And stored.

And the following are the streaks that ran down this column as Eric's words penetrated, as the laughter did not settle and fade, the way laughter is supposed to, but rather swelled and mounted in waves and rolled and rolled around me:

(1) The cruelty. He confessed affection after destroying utterly.

(2) The ridicule. I did not simply have a disease. I had *diseases*.

(3) The helplessness. The teacher's presence was as good as an endorsement.

(4) The humiliation. I was pitied even by the most pitiful.

(5) The shame. I was a Jordache wallet, so toxic that kindnesses in my direction had to be whispered.

(6) The degradation. I was no wallet—I was a squalid object to be stepped on, abased so that the formerly most pitiful might ascend.

(7) The treachery. Life itself had turned on me, had made possible my subjugation to a boy whose skin and bones I knew firsthand were built from a steady diet of congealed, pinky-picked mucus, had allowed the stretching of this moment, this scene, that though acute should have been finite, into an epoch of impossible length.

Every one of these streaks for itself.

Exactly one week later I was in the school cafeteria after dismissal. I had business at the vending machine because strawberry chews were reliable things that never betrayed. And as I turned out of the vending machine alcove into the side hallway, I saw a boy and a girl, kissing, the boy coolly possessive, hands around the small of the girl's back, one hand holding the other at the wrist so that the other was left to drape casually toward where it wanted to be.

Eric and Alison were kissing.

I stopped and watched wonderingly. Was he forcing himself on her? Her hands were on him. Was this a joke she was playing? There was no one else around. They didn't even know I was there.

They broke off. Alison saw me immediately. And without a word or any indication to Eric, she walked quickly away. Eric looked in my direction. He didn't really register a reaction either. And rather than follow Alison, he went out the side door.

The next day, in class, I caught Alison's eye. I blew a kiss at her. Her face crumpled.

For the next week, Alison Derby made no fun of me. For the next week, Alison Derby and Eric Trudd were a secret.

But this squalid object was not content to trade silence for accommodation. There was something about this tacit arrangement that stank of Alison's control, of Sperry Top-Sider laces meticulously rubber-banded at home each night in such a way that, at school the next day, the loops would curve inward and touch and make a pair of large and knowing eyes. And on Valentine's Day, I brought in my own cupcakes. This was before (in fact, kind of the reason behind) the prohibition at St. Mary's on students bringing in homemade treats without an accompanying parent.

By the time I got to class, with all the cupcakes handed out and pointed at and laughed about, I saw Alison Derby's chair empty. She wasn't out sick. I'd seen her from across the schoolyard as the boys battled for the last chocolate-frosteds because people talk about liking vanilla but come on. When she realized what was happening, likely at around the same time I was called to the principal's office, she went straight home.

I tried to imagine her lying on her living room couch as I sat on one of the hard chairs outside the principal's office, the column inside me made of the same wavy, pebbly glass in the principal's door, sweet glory streaming down one side and fear trickling thinly down the other. I was unprepared to explain why all the cupcakes I'd brought to school bore the same frosted message.

Alison

♡

Eric

The only true explanation was hardly straightforward:
      I had become Alison Derby.
      I remained Alison Derby—scheming, hurtful, frankly a little out of my mind—until a couple of months later. This was when, in one of the lucky oddities that collect along life's timeline like gleaming beads on a chain, the real Alison moved away. Some combination of Alison's departure and Billy Joel's *Glass Houses* saved me, or at least gave me the space to restore who I'd been.
      I will not tell you all the things I did in those two months. I prefer to believe that youth and circumstance were responsible and that I should not blame myself for doing the things I did to others and to my shoelaces.
      Eric Trudd's father died years ago. The upholstery shop has been shuttered for nearly two decades. Eric, however, owns an electronics store. He sells phones and audio equipment and sound systems for cars. He also sells two-headed robots and remote-controlled eels—these specialty items all store-made, the co-creations of Eric and his staff of one. I have been inside the store five or six times. I am compelled there by the recurring need for last-minute gifts. Many of these trips come just before the holidays—fortuitous timing because it justifies the excessive things I bake and bring with me: cakes with double frosting; chocolate-lake cookies with no chips, just a middle composed entirely of chocolate, large and

close enough to the perimeter that it offers itself to every bite; log flumes, composed of upright columns of almond brittle with alternating drizzles of white and dark chocolate down the sides; nutellow brownies, bisected by a proprietary mix of one company's chocolate hazelnut spread and another's marshmallow spread, so thoroughly stolen there can be nothing proprietary about them but Goddy are they good.

I do not bake anymore, except before trips to Eric Trudd's electronics store.

The treats are not for Eric—though each time I go, Eric looks so genuinely happy to see me that you'd think they were. They are for his son, currently eight years old. When this boy is not in school, he is the proprietor's sole staff person. Jerry is a miniature version of his father—hair and eyebrows of identical tint and texture, a way of listening with his mouth open as if he is so eager to hear what you're saying that he's putting extra face parts on the job—and this homunculus stands much too close to customers and says things that are odd but not quite bizarre and that depend on their vexingly equivocal status between these to compound the discomfort.

"I don't really get hot, but sometimes my legs get hot." This is one thing he says.

"What's your name? I'm Ronald. Just kidding. I'm Zack." His name, of course, is Jerry.

"Is there anything you like in here? If there's anything you don't like, I don't want to hear about it." This he likes to say deadpan, clearly copying something he once heard his father say, and the double contrivance—the witticism not only scripted but imitated—is painful to hear.

I look at the other customers chortling genuinely at the things he says. I watch them acting like everything is super okay, and it makes me feel worse.

Which is why I know that Jerry's favorite class is a tie between music and computers, and that Jerry wants a dog but Dad is allergic and Jerry is betting that a Bouvier is just hyperallergenic enough to fit the bill ("Hypo," I corrected him, but he just kept talking), and that the darker the chocolate, the more psyched the Jerry.

Why do I, a grown woman with husband and career and contentment, concern myself with a boy I have no reason to know? Things—relationships included—exist for a reason. Now, the mind's next move is to assume they exist for reasons having to do with us. But life teaches that is not true. Not true at all. That is arrogance. Things do not revolve around us.

And yet they do. Life teaches they do. Jerry is there to test me. He is there to goad me and to shrive me, to remind me of my continuing inhumanity—which is to say, my humanity. I am a good person. But that also is arrogance, and perhaps the supreme arrogance of life—thinking we have a fix on who we are, when all we can do is hearten the best parts of ourselves and hem in the lesser ones.

Last I heard, Alison Derby had given birth to two enormous babies and was living with her parents.

MR. AMBROSIO IS AN IDIOT

Mr. Ambrosio in N252 says if you hold your breath long enough, you'll pass away. He admits this does nothing for most people, swears and swears it works for those of extreme age. "The superannuated," he says, show-off. Not true. That is the plan of a child, she is sure. Mr. Ambrosio is an idiot, she is sure.

Men have the heart problems. Women have estrogen in their corner. But she was the one diagnosed with a heart problem at age forty-eight. She had every right to go before he did. These medications, they list every side effect. Except keeping you hardy for five funerals a month.

J.T.'s the one who keeps her swimming in pills. Nice as can be and asks lots of questions, and when she says "secondary insomnia" and lets her voice crack a little, he doesn't stand a chance. Once she saw his name on a staff manifest and knows it's not J.T. It's Juan Tobar Encarnación. She's the only one who calls him Juan. The only challenge is to remember to save them, and to hide them well, because really he doesn't stand a chance.

Her grandchildren sometimes visit on Saturdays. And Sundays. Almost never on Saturdays or Sundays.

But it's possible they could come on a Sunday. So she'll do it on a Monday because that leaves the most time until their next visit. No sense in their getting caught by surprise. Or—yes. Time for arrangements and notifications. Because that would be cruel, wouldn't that be cruel?

The pills are small. Thirty-four white pills she can handle. Lord knows she's been training for years with fourteen, fifteen a day. Their last vacation together was in Denver, Colorado. They both got lightheaded from the elevation. The roof on that airport had thirty-four white peaks representing the Rocky Mountains. It would be nice to swallow them forever. Monday.

The woman in the bed across from her has shoulder-length hair and sleeps day and night. They're always letting in the Jehovah's Witnesses. They are very, very, very nice women, but what business do they have going into people's rooms? These are their homes. They ask, "What's her name?" Both names are right there on the placard on the hallway wall, just below the room number, but she humors them. "They need to cut Vivian's hair," the unsmiling one says. "Vivian looks like a jungle woman," the smiling one says.

Forget Mr. Ambrosio. This is the secret. What you do is hold your breath while thinking of how much you've lost. Now that works. You can't stop breathing long enough to think of everything. So you fail, and you pant. And sitting there, a sweating, panting failure, you're as human and alive as you ever were.

THE SISTERS JEPPARD

My cousin married a woman who was an only child. Her mother had two sisters. These aunts had no children of their own.

The three sisters all treated this woman, my cousin's wife, as their daughter. In her youth she was dandled and spoiled and trophied. The three sisters were her regents, she their queen. This is all from my cousin. I didn't know her when she was growing up. Neither did he. They went to the same middle school, my cousin and his wife, but they ran with different sets of kids. They got genuinely acquainted only a couple of years ago, his mother bumping into her mother at Lord & Taylor. He knew the family dynamic from bits and pieces: things she told him, things friends and relatives told him, not being blind.

She grew up to be an engaging person and thoughtful. This I can report. But also moody, and prone to self-involvement, and fond of spending money and nursing wounds and spending money to nurse wounds. She saw catastrophe in the merest challenges. In all the time I knew her, she never asked me a question.

She laughed rarely, never at things I said. Once, I suggested she come up with a new origin story for the grandchildren. They would be like, What's Lorden Tailor?, and she'd be like, A store at the mall, and they'd be like, What's a mall?, and of course no matter what she said they wouldn't get it, Retail? What's a retail?, etcetera, and unless her grandchildren were French absurdists, this infinite regression would not satisfy. That's what I said, French absurdists and infinite regression, and she gave me a look you give orphans with rabies.

Her upbringing, so different from how the hard world handles a person, likely shaped these habits of character. And maybe explained why she and my cousin broke up. It didn't much explain what came after.

The youngest of the three sisters worked at a museum. She was so shy I dreaded seeing her at holiday parties and family dinners. Our greet hug seemed amutual, like I was subjecting her to something. She spoke softly and chirpily: a girl wondering about candy. Her face was very white and her hair and eyes very dark. I expected her to blush when speaking with me and my husband and kids—the encounter always seemed to find her jarred and exquisitely uncertain, and the months that invariably had passed since last we'd met may have stripped from her a coherent feeling of familiarity to match the expectation of familiarity, and that snowy skin seemed so color-susceptible—but she never blushed. Instead she held her head at a canting angle that, like a carnival ride, lent itself to a long and fast swing away.

The middle sister had a Chesterfield sofa in her living room, the whole bit: traditional quilted leather, pair of seat cushions. Twice I saw her sit right in the middle, over the cleft between the cushions, though nobody else was on the sofa. Maybe she did this out of hospitality, to leave open the choicest seats. In ancient times the hosts parceled out to guests the thighs and cheeks of spitted animals, and this one plopped her cheeks and thighs down at couch's center. Maybe not hospitality, maybe aberration: what would compel a person to arrange herself in such a way that effectively she was sitting on precisely nothing? She was a doctor—an anesthesiologist—and had a mouth that opened wide for the vowels and a voice that blared. Without a doubt she was the loudest of the sisters. The maxim among anesthesiologists is that putting patients to sleep is easy; only the waking is tricky. With that voice like a bugle corps, it stood to reason she was a mandarin in the field. She needed neither art nor chemistry to rouse her patients, or the dead, or the night-slumbering villages of Papua New Guinea from the cozy remove of her Duchess County home. Just talking.

The oldest sister—my cousin's mother-in-law—was a protocol engineer, or a data builder, or something else where the noun is concrete but the modifier abstract. People with occupations like that, you look and look to glimpse something correspondingly wizardy about them, but good luck. She was certainly kind, always making an effort, always asking in the run-up to some get-together what the kids might like for dessert, and she didn't have to do that. Her voice was like sun through a scratched window, warm and frayed. She was in her sixties and likely had sounded like she was in her sixties since her twenties. It was a voice of diverse capacities, a gentle lilt in easy discourse and a stridency that crawled up the back of your skull in loud cross-kitchen exchanges. When she wanted to compete with the middle sister for conversational position, she'd ratchet up the volume to an indignant scrape, and the first time I heard her raise her voice—not out of anger, she was joking, but she was making sure she was heard—was when I realized I'd heard it many, many times before. Her voice was a violin. The tone, the range, the warmth and fickleness: all like a violin. The resemblance made satisfying sense. It wasn't just the texture and heterogeneity of the sounds she made. It was the neat complement to the truth that her younger sisters were a flute and a trumpet. This trio of sisters was the classic ensemble: woodwind, brass, and string.

Now, when they got loud, these voices turned philharmonic. And three orchestral sections imply the missing fourth. Maybe this occurred to you, just now? Not me. It took a couple of months before I thought of it. Once the idea entered my head, though, it never left. Every holiday party, I'd walk in and hear the sisters, and I'd think, Where is the percussion? Every family dinner, I'd sit down and reflexively remove the knives from the kids' place settings, and monitoring the chatter and waiting for the rolls to come around, I'd wonder, Where is the percussion?

Once married, cousin and wife moved into a house fairly sweet. The three sisters made sure of that. The oldest sister bought for their dining room a pairing of concrete and abstract: chandelier plus installation. The youngest sister found a small pew, salvaged from a church, that slotted alongside the front door with the kind of custom-fit serendipity that suburbanites count as a miracle. And the middle sister had a deep-buttoned Chesterfield delivered, one just like hers, except the cushions with their jutting edges needed years of leg-curing to slope pleasingly instead. But these weren't enough. My cousin's wife bought more and more, filled the house with more. Accent pieces and wall hangings, matching sets and ancillaries. Half-moon tables whose stark abruption suggested continuation past the abutted walls into another, better dimension. The basement was an orchid show of turned-out boxes and packaging pollen, all of it kept assiduously in case of returns. There were never returns.

My cousin sickened of the heaps of shapes on the front steps, of the figures that leered from the bottoms of their credit card statements, of the way she spiked their weekends with obligations that included only her: salon appointments and personal training sessions and lunches with friends. They tried marriage counseling, but she did not change. When the world consists of infinite nurture and seats you at its center, there's just no reason not to proceed high and untrammeled. He told her he was leaving her. When she refused to believe it, he moved out of the house. When he sent her the names and numbers of divorce attorneys, she responded with the names and numbers of other marriage counselors.

It got so that whenever my cousin visited what was now, functionally, his wife's house—to visit their three dogs, to take away belongings some boxes at a time—he was sure to ask me or my husband to come along. He did not want entanglement in the strange counterfactual world she conjured aloud each time she saw him, musings and wandering elegies about their times together and sometimes bright smiles and sometimes tears. She was hefting a net of regrets around this man. It didn't work.

One Saturday he and I came to the house for his bike and his living room books, my husband home with the kids, and she'd drunk drain cleaner. The door was ajar. For all we know she might have swallowed it just moments before, maybe even as she'd heard us pull into the driveway. We found her curled up in the right rear corner of the Chesterfield, coughing. The dogs were crazed and barking, running outside and inside and outside again, keeping away from the couch and unable to keep away. They knew. She sensed us and stirred and stared, no alarm or desperation, her eyes a question, shifting from her husband to me and back. She couldn't say anything, though. Couldn't talk. She was coughing and coughing. Staring at us and coughing up red and thin. We didn't know for a dense minute what was happening. My cousin called 911. I went to her, and I should have held her, but I was asking her things instead—What's wrong, what's happening. Really just barking like one of the dogs. Coughing, she held up a wavering hand in the direction of nothing. Eventually I saw it: on the carpet by her end of the couch, on its side and spilled, a jug thing of drain cleaner with a festive label.

Eventually my cousin remarried. By then he'd aged well past his age: scalp pinking and patching between the hairs, movements slowed—droopy, even—his words too. Widowers and widows know that, hurry or not, anything at all can happen by the time they get to the end of a sentence, or a house's front walk, or a remembering. No dogs. He had two rascally, furless kids, both boys. He and I grabbed coffee every three months. I made sure to schedule it like a quarterly release of earnings, rigid and official as possible, so he couldn't put off getting together out of sheepishness just because we both knew that after the light jokes and the family updates, he'd only say the same thing to me, over and over, knowing it imparted nothing and would gain him nothing. Why? he'd repeat, not looking especially at me.

You've thought of it already. Or you're thinking of it now. But this wasn't the percussion. Her coughing wasn't the percussion, if that's what you were thinking. No. Nor his asking why, why.

It wasn't the rat-tat-tat laughter in which one autumn evening I saw the youngest of the sisters indulge with what looked like a friend while the two stood outside a movie theater, or the few moments thereafter when I pulsed with sudden hatred a few feet from this docent sister because her niece was dead and how could she, or the next moments when, catching myself, I pulsed with astonished shame for feeling something so ballistic and unfair and hurried away.

It wasn't years later when the phone rang and rang and it was one of those cute, furless kids, the unsmiling older one who people said had grown into a jerk, who informed me his dad, my cousin, had been in a car wreck. The accident hadn't killed him. But he died nonetheless because later, as we waited at the hospital, the surgeon came out and told us an artery had been nicked during surgery and they hadn't caught it in time. It wasn't the way the surgeon held his hands stiffly in front of him, fingers folded and heels and knuckles touching, like two gray blocks he was preparing to knock together, or the way he said these implausible things—nicked? a nick?—with such bizarre slowness it reminded me of how my cousin himself had spoken. This doctor, well cologned and shoulders like a parade float, was in agony.

It's not now, years later, as I sit here at the funeral of my cousin's second wife, who became my best friend in the world. A teenager I don't recognize talks too close to the mic. The leaflet says it's a reading, a Kazantzakis selection. What I hear is a pubescent half-yodel and the PBOFF PBOFF PBOFF of his super-amplified lips. Oppressive. If we were dice and this church a cup, it's what God's blowing would sound like. I know she's being cremated, and yet at the front of the room reigns a casket of scroll-carved mahogany, dome-roofed and massive. My cousin's other son, the younger one, the one known for kindness and charm, rented this show coffin—it's a thing people do, apparently, to focus the room and thicken the ritual—in lieu of flying home from Indonesia. It's the older one who has prepared the reflection we're due to hear after Kazantzakis and who, before the service, as I entered alone, looked up and promptly abandoned the minister and a little talking clutch of people to guide me to a front pew and watch as I settled myself and ask if I wanted water.

It was these together. These surprises, disconnections, the rhythm of the world flinging itself successively into us—we who pretended we had it mastered. Oh, we didn't, we don't. Like mastering a blind and leggy mule. Whether we understand it, whether we learn from it or decide resolutely to improve from it, it doesn't care. The second-to-last funeral I attended was my husband's. I stood at the dessert table nodding and nodding again, well-wishers drifting toward, crooning bromides, drifting out, drifting toward. My kids, one fewer than we raised because septicemia, like the world, doesn't mind how hard you hope, stood on either side of me, attentive, crooning back. Around our diminished little rank of three wrapped the special squalor of other, actual children scampering indoors in dress clothes, jagging and squealing and tripping. I looked down. Resting on the top of my right foot was a little paper plate, abandoned by one of these children. On top of that: an untouched, caterer-style half slice of cheesecake. My first thought was not how irrelevant I must have seemed to the young perpetrator, my brittle progress and wholesale lack of intent making me seem more like a discard tray than a living thing. My first thought, seeing no graham cracker crust, was that the child had nothing to answer for.

How do you blame those sisters for giving their girl every love, for knowing that the world is unrelenting and that the young need a commensurately maximum devotion? I'd do the same. Looking back, knowing what I know, I'd do exactly the same. God bless them for doing as if they'd been certain when they could not have been. Nothing about her dying was good, and her dying gave me the best friend I ever had. The three sisters, they are long gone, and their staunch love is our subject still. We know so little.

Here is the percussion, these beats the world gives to show that these lives are not our own, that they are contingent and slight. A rain of rocks, more or less, and bewilderment. Go ahead and look up, or look down, it doesn't matter. It doesn't matter if we dodge smartly, cheer a little when the drops fall wide, give up, give thanks.

The only comfort is the idea, strictly notional, of shelter somewhere. Three embracing mothers better than one, and solace where banks of proud leather come to a corner. The dark and the hush.

MIGHTY SEVEN

Mighty Seven. He loves the Seven. Almost always running. Almost always get a seat. Feels right too. You go upstairs to fly, you come down to walk the earth. Five continents on one train, staring back at you through every kind of face. Costume ball, and it does not end at midnight. God all giddy by the sixth day.

He climbs the station stairs from the street. Handrail splits the middle. He climbs up the wrong side. The left side. Okay, but the right side of the left side.

At the top of the stairs. Right there. A starlet. What else do you call somebody shining like that, holding a MetroCard, making everyone pass by wish they were that MetroCard, and carrying drops of sweat on her nose. Those drops don't look like dew or jewels. They look like sweat. It's just she makes sweat look good. Like a present you wish you had. Her eyes are dark moons. By the sixth day God knew exactly what the fuck.

She starts down but, seeing him hog the stairs, goes skittish. That foot dipping down to the top step, she takes that foot and brings it back and puts it around the base of the handrail to the other side. She's thinking about him. About the stairs, sure, but she's made a decision and it's about him.

Kind of a miracle and it makes him feel good. Kind of sorry for scaring off beauty instead of treating it tender and it makes him feel bad. Both make him feel stupid for thinking stupid shit and when he shakes it off something breaks off at the mouth. Words.

"I'll make room for you," he says. He knows to push the "I'll" for friendliness. He knows to smile with his lips closed so she doesn't think he wants something, his eyebrows down so she doesn't think he's a whack job, his eyes warm so he looks like someone's brother.

She surprises him. The moons go narrow, those moons are setting, and she purrs, "No, I'll make room for you." Purrs this. She knows to push the "you" for sass. She smiles. Not like someone's sister.

They move by each other, both looking past their three o'clocks, but whatever and then she's out of sight.

One year later he's in the same station but climbing different stairs. The higher ones, the ones from the turnstiles to the platform. On the right side of the left side because it's the least bad of his bad habits. Wait. At the top of the stairs. It's her. Coming down. Cut her hair. She's with a man. The type with clothes all figured out, the type who could be lost because this isn't Brooklyn.

He ignores her friend and catches her eye.

"I'll make room for you," he says.

She looks at him, her eyes bigger than the moons he remembers, her mouth says, "What?" but she hangs on to his face, with that dumb look between wondering and wonder. The moment they pass each other, she snaps out of it and puts her lips hard and says, "Change your shirt."

What are you going to do and she's gone.

Her eyes stayed soft.

Can it be the same shirt as a year ago? No. He bought it years ago. Two years ago. Best shirt for warm muggy days. Days like this one. Days like the one a year ago.

Yeah. Yes, it is the same shirt.

Five years later, he steps on a subway car. She steps off. He nearly slams into her because one of them's not keeping to the right. She is alone. Her hair falls past her shoulders. Makes everyone pass by wish they could swim in that hair. She is not alone. She pushes a stroller. She is not alone because in that stroller is a fat, bug-eyed baby with one sock on and one sock off.

"I'll make room for you," he says.

She's concentrating on doors and chubby feet, but she tumbles out of that when she sees him. She puts her lips soft. Her eyes do not disappoint either.

"You're hopeless," she mouths through the closing doors.

Mighty Seven. He hates the Seven. Goddamn exhausting train. Does not let him rest. He is watchful, always on the lookout. Years he has not seen her. One of these with the caps and laughing like they know, one of these could be that fat, bug-eyed baby. Whatever. What are you going to do. He is always alert, always watchful, proving a stranger wrong.

GROSSNESS

Sunday night. Late enough that we have to be quick.
Cass has school tomorrow. We need to get back
home by, more or less, now.

But Grossness takes time. Mostly because Cass
will not be rushed. At Grossness, at anything. She is a
consummate operator. Don't be fooled by those wide
whorls of pale green. Eyes like her mom's. They advertise
simplicity, but behind them work vast intricacies,
quirking and stamping in perfect quiet like the latest
machines. She revels—*revels*—in the spotlight that
competition imparts. Is her voice the chirp of sweetest
mornings? Sure. Yes. And that voice, please know, is
how a conqueress throws opponents off their game.

All this means the opposite of quick.

It's so late that it's too dark to read the plaque outside.
You wouldn't even know there was a plaque outside.
Since when do Shop Rites have plaques outside? The
plaque says they built St. Patrick's Cathedral in New
York City with stone quarried from the site that is
now the hole in which this supermarket sits. The store,
for its part, is content to leave this unconfirmed and
undenied. It merely shines like a god-baby, squat and

lit up from within, contemplating the world with a calm cheer from inside its granite mandorla. It radiates the signature contradictory attitude of divine things: at once oblivious of all the trivial that is chaff and highly, highly aware, with a pitying intelligence, of all the trivial that matters.

You can still see the walls of unquarried stone that loom behind the store. The gouges and jags visible up and down the rock face are lasting insults. No one bothered to smooth or polish, to put aright, after wresting what they wanted. These jags and gouges suggest a larger order of magnitude, like they were etched by a giant with the pointy end of a bridge. That's the physical dynamic. That's not the metaphysical dynamic. The metaphysical dynamic is that pieces of the thirteenth most famous religious building in the world were once pieces of the very cubic space composing this Shop Rite. Put differently, there is a one-to-one correspondence between each place where inside this refrigerated mega-box you might reach for frozen spinach soufflé, say, or bump shopping carts with the travel-team soccer coach, and each place where earlier this morning, thirty-one miles away, at the corner of Fifth Avenue and Fiftieth Street, you might have reached for a Bible and turned without knowing it to the book of Obadiah or tried to ignore all the tourists, knowing full well you were one of them.

You'd think these were facts that deserved a plaque with dedicated lighting.

The Shop Rite is near empty. I know this from the parking lot. Also the deli counter. Mrs. Searles (name tag) stares from behind it. Usually she disdains eye contact altogether. She barks out, "Next," handles the provolones like they're back from furlough with ideas, asks if you want Boar's Head or store brand, grunts. Mrs. Searles has been here for years, used to get into it with Cass's mom because Norah never remembered to take a numbered ticket and would refuse to get skipped over and would let Mrs. Searles know she couldn't pretend they weren't all just human beings. But tonight Mrs. Searles rests her head and face on her folded arms upon the counter and hovers her stare over whatever passes by. Her hands are still gloved in plastic. The gloves are both see-through and transparent: a show of readiness that says, *Don't blame me I got nothing to do.* In fairness, Mrs. Searles doesn't look like she plans on drooling. She looks like, were the prospect of drooling to occur to her, she'd be fully fine with it.

Cass, gone hunting for grossness, stalks back toward me with her finds. She's got both hands behind her back and all the breezy subtlety of tracked armor. Her lips are wrestling with each other. Either she's fighting down a smile or she's finding it a challenge to carry merchandise behind herself.

"Here, Daddy."

"What's this?'

Bottle of yellow mustard. Cratelet of pre-cut watermelon.

"Nicely done," I say. "Mustard watermelon. Gross."

"No. Chunks of watermelon in mustard soup."

"Even grosser. That'll be tough to top."

"Yeah," says Cass. She's released herself to smile, showing off the twin gaps where incisors used to hang. "Darla Ippolito says girls' brains make connections that boys' brains don't."

"Like, their brains work faster?"

"No. They work better. Girls' brains think more things than boys' brains. And you're a boy. So, dot dot dot."

Fanglessness is a universal trait of her age group. Maybe it's an evolutionary device, signaling to bigger specimens an eagerness to coexist. *I may be growing up and cute-ing down,* those blank gums say, *but with a bite like this I'm definitely not a threat.*

"What's dot dot dot?" I say.

"You know, like, when you don't say what comes next, but you kinda know."

"Does Darla say dot dot dot?"

"No. You don't know what three dots mean?"

"I do, but—did you make that up?" I keep the cart moving and my eyes on the shelves. This will leaven the intensity of my curiosity, elicit maximum information. "Or do your friends say that?"

"I made it up."

"Sure, okay."

I think about coaster brakes and how strange it is to put your face against the other side of a window as it's being washed and three movies with scarabs. That should make enough of a pause.

"But did you see somebody on YouTube say dot dot dot?" I continue. "Or maybe one of your classmates likes to say it."

I look over. Too much. I have achieved the breezy subtlety of tracked armor.

"No, Daddy." She's standing on tiptoes, so keen is she to help me understand. "I said dot dot dot because I know what it means. Not because other people say it."

The single-instance past tense—"said"—lends credibility. I stand down. It's my own background worry. She shouldn't have to deal with it. I worry that she's roaming the internet too freely, that she's spending too much time staring at screens. That when she's not staring at screens, she's subjected to Taylor and Moraya, the mean girls in her class. They're not mean like they carry knives, but they're mean like they wage weird campaigns of social manipulation, inventing elaborate games that trap the other kids in a choice between obeying Tayaya's every command ("Tayaya" being their own coinage, apparently; one wonders what depraved enticement Taylor offered Moraya to secure top billing) and conspicuously excluding themselves from the group. Also, they talk about other girls' weight *at age seven*. I almost wish Tayaya carried knives. I could just give Cass and Darla Ippolito longer knives. Norah was able to draw Cass out just by putting her mouth a certain way, by keeping silent exactly the right number of moments. Everybody's got a different style. I have my own style. My style is ponderous, forced. Many fathers lack a fundamental grace. Have you noticed this? Or maybe it's just the single parents, trying so hard to keep things together that all people see is the trying and not the together.

The Sunday-night regulars are the lords of the Shop Rite. There are so few of them, all roughly the same age: past the middle years but short of great-grandparent eligibility. The way they move they've got a lot of nerve. Closer to death and yet *less* in a hurry—and by choice because their bodies have not yet buckled and forced a structural slowness. The Shop Rite at night is their domain. If you had your pick of domains, could you do much better than the Shop Rite? Vast open lanes ahead and behind for the wandering. Small bright objecterie at both flanks for the palpating. Incandescence all around.

Tonight my daughter and I are the trespassers. We know the Sunday-night supermarket is for the non-elderly old. We are not yet that. Cassandra is seven. I am forty-eight. Shut up. Forty-eight is still, very fairly, in middle age. Forty-eight is not old. Seriously, shut up.

Mr. Donny (name tag) is stacking plastic-wrapped meats into the coolers. He resembles a gym-teacher impersonator. That is, he looks more like a gym teacher than most gym teachers. Body lean, clothing kempt, face good for burning indelible memories. This last is iconically strange, with ball-of-yarn eyebrows and a nose like a galleon's prow. He works at speed, as if a crowd of shoppers surges behind him, shrieking his name, mad for the next London broil to drop. Alongside him sits a special cart made of confusing polybutylene: bread-thick and round-cornered like it was engineered for day care but in a foreboding gray. He plucks two bubbles of blood off the cart, faces us as he does so, turns and negotiates where these packages will cozy down for the night, then faces us again for two more packages. His movements are so brief and twitchy that when I follow them with my eyes and pretend in my head like I'm moving just as he's moving, I get nauseous.

"Hiya," says Mr. Donny, without looking, without stopping. And then he looks—at Cass, not me.

"Is Daddy behaving himself?" he says. "Is Daddy being a good helper?"

Cass smiles, shrugs.

"Okay," he says. "Let me know if that changes. All right? All right."

With that, Mr. Donny dives back into his work. Cass looks up at me, still smiling, but now with eyes squinted in derisive confusion and a quizzical mouth slightly open. I shrug back.

"He's got a time-out room back there," I say, loud enough for Mr. Donny to hear. "It's cold."

Mr. Donny doesn't react. To get Mr. Donny's attention, it seems, one must be either alive and young or dead and plastic-wrapped.

We mush the shopping cart across the sprawl of floor. This floor is hard for a reason: to hold up against the constant grind of cart wheels. This floor is white for a reason: to set off in starkest contrast the stain of beef blood and the spill of blueberry yogurt, thus spurring the worker to clean these and reassuring the customer that the likes of these have been cleaned.

On Sunday nights, however, come superseding orders. The floor is hard for a different reason: to announce the presence and progress of intruders. Cass's footsteps and mine sound like a tap-and-jazz recital at a bowling alley. The floor is white for a new and urgent reason: to set off in starkest contrast the progress of intruders. Cass and I *are* the beef blood—untoward, unwanted. The geniuses talk of paving the roads with solar cells. Shop Rite, uncelebrated, has managed to pave the ground with gory bell.

The organics aisle is the easiest for Grossness. The miscellany there of foods not otherwise found in proximity makes it easy to find two that pair revoltingly. Is the happenstance of my turn coinciding with the organics aisle a bit of an unfair advantage? Yes. Do I have a problem with that? Not especially. Do *you* like losing to seven-year-olds? That's what I thought.

"Here you go," I say, handing over my chosen items.

This is one of my secret strategies. I physically transfer the items rather than just show them. I figure there is a prestige to possession in this world of fleeting things. At a subconscious level, surely, a person is less likely to defame the worth of a thing she holds herself.

"Granola bars and salsa," she says, unimpressed.

"Gross, right?"

"Eh," she says, staunch in her unimpressedness. Kids do not grow up gradually. Kids grow up suddenly, acutely, in those moments calculated by fate to make their parents feel most ridiculous.

"Come on," I say. "That's gross."

"*I'd* eat it."

My secret strategy is mostly just a secret.

"No, you wouldn't."

"On a desert island I would."

"On a desert island I'd eat watermelon-crouton mustard soup."

"No, you wouldn't."

"On a desert island I'd lick my coconut shell clean. I'd hide from every rescue boat if I had enough watermelon-crouton mustard soup."

"Daddy."

"Unless of course the boats were loaded with more mustard-melon soup. Yummers."

"*You're* a mustard-melon soup."

That's my girl. One moment she grows up. The next moment she regresses to her homuncula self, composed entirely of cartilage and silly sass.

We're making good time. Only a few customers purl down the aisles. They're obligated to complete the length of each before moving to the next. Unlike the

newer stores, this one features no widthwise passage
cutting the aisles in half. Old-school footprint, old-
school commitment. Now and then, the customers
reach absently for the shelves. If you were to tie freshly
wetted paintbrushes to their ankles, you'd never see a
stripe. You'd see only spreading pools from the standstill
sopping. Their desultory pace resembles nature. That's
how shoppers steal for themselves a sneaky dignity.
They're shoppers, they're not scientists or clerics or
presidents. Well, some of them may be, granted. But
none of them in a supermarket is titrating suspensions
or leading prayers or mulling fresh intel. They're just
shopping. Yet shoppers always manage to seem so
measured and self-possessed. And that's their secret.
They ape nature. They mimic her regal and fated and
incomprehensible processes. Consequently, they look
like queens and kings. Mysterious. Inevitable. Some
kinds of misbehavior are hardly punished.

If this store had a widthwise passage, it would
coincide with the cathedral's nave.

I hand her one item.

"Where's the other thing?" she says.

"What do you mean?" I say.

"This is salt. Morton Salt, it says."

"Yes."

"But you need two things."

She doesn't know what my second item is. She
knows it won't be salt. It was Norah who came up with
the two-of-a-kind move. Two vats of vanilla pudding.
Two family-size bags of Funyuns. It was a pleasing
absurdity: the non-surprise surprise of an identical
item, the notion of sheer excess being disgusting. We
don't play Norah's move.

Both things are of her. The game as a whole, the
two-of-a-kind move. She suffuses both things. One we
play always, exactly because. The other we play never,
exactly because. Why? I don't know. I should probably
just ask Cass. Better yet, don't put the burden on her. Just

tell her why I don't do the move, without waiting for it to come up, after I figure out why I don't. Such a small thing. It'll sound casual, not a big deal. Communication, positivity, time. I remember the counselor at the hospital very well. Mostly his breath like a box left out in the damp. But also his condescension, his clearly well-intentioned condescension, which meant you couldn't get fed up with him, or maybe you could. His shtick about our three best tools. Those are your tools, he said. Use your tools. Well, time's easy enough. Time happens. You can't screw that up. But communication? Sure, there's no downside to it when you just say it like that, the last syllable delivered with a knowing puff smelling of moldering cardboard. But communication in the moment. When you go to tuck her in and she's desperate to hide that she's been crying. When you want positivity so badly for her that the slightest risk of communication ruining everything is abhorrent, and so fuck communication. What about that?

I produce the second item from behind my back with an extravagance generally reserved for objects bearing magic runes.

"A spoon," she says.

"Yes, a spoon," I say. "Salt, and a big plastic spoon to eat it all with."

It's a red plastic serving spoon. Eight or ten times the size of a tablespoon. The color and caricaturish size suggest the only way to eat a twenty-six-ounce helping of salt is to fall upon it ravenously.

"That's gross," she says. "That's extremely gross, Daddy. Daddy, I think you won."

A hundred thousand items in this store. Two thousand humans in and out of it every day. None of them compares with this waist-high sprite bursting at the skull seams with tangled curls. She will concede defeat, even when victory means the world to her. With that heart of hers, so good, so obliviously and unquestioningly good, honesty and kindness are the same thing.

This is one of the thousand reasons I love her like an acetylene torch.

"I don't know, girl. If anybody can beat me, it's you."

It's quiet. I've knocked out all but four items on the shopping list. I find one of the four further up the aisle. If I double back—yep, there it is. I'm down to two. I'm feeling both calm and masterful. And that's when I remember: danger signs. These are danger signs. No parent of a young child gets to feel calm and masterful. Cass. Where is she?

I motor down Aisle 11 with the cart, thinking maybe she's behind the mac and cheese display that juts out from the shelves like a Huck Finn island. Nope. Nothing.

"Dad!"

Behind me. I pull a U-turn.

"Where'd you go?" I say. She's dragging behind her a very large art pad.

"Next aisle."

"I thought the rule was you have to pick from the aisle you're in."

"Yeah," she says. "But you said we had time for one more turn. So I thought I'd go quick to the next aisle."

I feel a little bad. Aisle 12, the next aisle and also the second-to-last of all, is the ultimate slumgullion: hampers and seasonal items and plastic flowers and mousetraps, plus a cooler that wraps around from Aisle 13 with the start of the dairy items. She has her work cut out for her.

She reads my look of sympathy as a look of doubt.

"It's got better stuff," she says, as if this is so obvious I should be held accountable for making her point it out.

"All right," I say. "Whatdya got?"

She leans the giant art pad against her hip so that she can hand me a quart of cottage cheese. She holds this with both hands far away from her, like a transplant nurse with an organ phobia.

"What's this?" I say.

She pauses, steely.

"Cottage cheese."

"Okay."

"With no spoon."

"Cottage cheese with no spoon. Okay."

"And this." She nudges her chin downward toward the giant pad.

"A drawing pad?"

She shakes her head. With one hand—deft, definitely breezy—she spins it around. It's not an art pad. It's a cheap tall mirror with a white chipboard backing. For door mounting.

"A mirror?"

"Yep," she says.

"So how is this gross?"

"Cottage cheese with no spoon."

"Okay?"

"You have to eat it. With no spoon. *In front of a mirror.*"

"That is—"

She watches me.

"That's like—" I say. "Damn!"

"Daddy!" She gets cross with me when I bite my nails. Also when I curse.

"Sorry. I mean—"

"You can eat it with your hands or just with your mouth," she says. "Supergross either way."

I walk over to the mirror, size it up. I lean it against the mac and cheese. I stand both of us in front of it, side by side.

"Ladies and gentlemen," I intone.

Long before anybody's wrist is held at championship height, or thrust up, or even grasped, the mirror shows a reverse-vampire grin.

We're on the tail end now. Momentum gathers, last aisle breached. It's empty, this last aisle. Not a single other shopper. Pure runway.

You know as well as I do that an opportunity like this cannot be wasted. I repeat: pure, unmitigated runway. Cass and I have to race. Open-air coolers on the left, glass-door freezers on the right. Winner is first to make it under the aisle sign dangling from the ceiling at the other end and reading "13" with a two-column mini-menu underneath:

Eggs	*Frozen Food*
Dairy	*Frozen Corn*
Juice	*Dessert*

Winner takes everything, which is to say, nothing, which is to say, a justification for both of us to prolong the giddiness of our championship moment, to laugh and laugh and lose it for a little longer, to get home way too late.

How could I have guessed that she'd fall?

With that slick floor, so hard, how could I not have guessed that she'd fall?

All fast and frantic, limbs flapping, that happy gaping face, an affront to supermarket calm, the opposite of nature and its placid inscrutability and infinite green and infinite eons: how could I not have guessed she'd be singled out for punishment?

I heard a sound when she fell.

The floor is hard for a reason: to make what's happening keep happening, it can't dissolve into anything else. To hold up against the wear of people running, crowding around, more than were in the store surely, where are they coming from? The supermarket manager on the phone. To announce their approach, to announce an error. To ape the surfaces of the world outside, unyielding, indifferent, it does nothing to help.

There's never a reason.

A sickening sound when she fell.

The floor is white for a reason: to set off in contrast so that even Cass's mother can see what's happening, makes two people who don't deserve this, she can see how grievously she's been failed.

There are no reasons. Just one thing after another, one aisle and then the next, and the stories we tell ourselves to keep up. That's the only reason. That's always the reason.

One future day, long after this day of calamity, Cass and I will shop quietly, impeccably, congratulate each other as we fit bags into the trunk, heavy ones first and cold to the right, we've got a system, on how quickly we got in and out of the store.

One future day, long after her day of calamity, Cass will emerge from her bedroom, where she will have retreated in a fury after accusing me of willfully misunderstanding the scope of her math project at multiple points during an excruciating hour-long study session, and say so cheerfully, as if none of that ever happened, as if math were tulle and tea ring cookies, and life an endless sun-washed plain of delights, "Daddy, you ready to rock the Shop Rite?"

One future day, long after our day of calamity, Cass and I will walk through the parking lot to the store entrance, and I'll be holding her other hand, the one that's not holding the car keys.

Mrs. Searles is here. Kneeling with me and helping. Mrs. Searles is here with us in the aisle. It would be the sanctuary, behind the altar. There's not that kind of urgency. She didn't need to come. It will be fine.

One future day, long after my day of calamity, I'll take Cass's son to Shop Rite. Just inside the entrance, I'll rest my hands gamely on the fronts of my thighs, doing my best impersonation of an amiable grandpa. *Now remember, no running,* I'll say, and he'll take off running. *No running,* I'll yell, and that thirty-pound terrorist will keep running. Somehow I'll catch up and get ahold of a warm, moist, doughy shoulder—like a turnover sweating out its butter—and turn his body around and say, as sternly as I can manage, *DO NOT RUN.*

I will ignore the wide whorls of green in that face. I will bend closer, and I will pause ominously—maybe, like his mother, I enjoy a spotlight—and I will shake my bald-but-for-the-bristle head and say, no-foolingly:

Boy child, what's your favorite ice cream? Chocolate, is it? Well, let's go buy some. Let's go buy some right now. Because if you continue to run, then we will bring home a brick of the stuff, and I will sit on one side of the kitchen table and you on the other, and you will watch me eat all your chocolate ice cream, every bit of it, with a big red plastic spoon, and before each slow and sloppy spoonful, I'll say:

"This one's because you ran."

"And this one's because you didn't stop running even after I told you to."

"And this one's because you made me run just to catch you, even though there's no running."

"And this one's because you have to learn your lesson about running."

And then, when I dig up one more spoon of ice cream, I'll say, "And what do you think this one's for?" And you'll say, "Running?" And I'll say, "Nope, not for running. It's for—oh, wait a second, yes. Yes, it is. It is for running."

And I'll eat that spoonful and the next and the next, and I'll keep eating till there's no more chocolate ice cream in Shop Rite or the tristate area or anywhere in the world. SO DON'T RUN.

And he'll look up at me, pop-eyed, holding one hand with the other out in front of his body like he can't decide between singing an aria and asking a question, and finally, opting for the latter, he'll ask, *Why not running?*

Mrs. Searles is holding her too. Mrs. Searles' hands on my hands. Let me have her. The supermarket manager knows, he's here, and Mr. Donny too . . .

FOR YOU, CITY, FOR YOU

He skims the east curb. His skin is ambiguous, the color of a wallet. Perhaps he brought it from another continent. Perhaps he simply enjoyed sports as a child.

There are emissions, do not doubt it: from right rear, a spongy squeak like stale popcorn fighting; from underneath, something metal and cantankerous. He stands easy on the pedals.

On the sidewalk the slow ones look down, the fast ones forward. There is a different vernal equinox, lasting three days or four, very sweet, during which there are tourists enough that they are picked out instantly but not so many that tracking them makes him dizzy. It has come and well gone. The clouds wheel on him a little.

At the next intersection, two girls. They put their bodies in a way that wants to show they do not depend on each other. He slows. They are on his left as he approaches. His shoulders are back and relaxed and challenging. The girls look up but not at him. On a volume basis, his gaze is the least returned in the city.

The first girl he passes, the northerly, looks at last. But now she lifts her hand to her chest and waggles and drops it. She does this as if to say, Look, you know the drill, you know we do not want a ride in your pedicab, you know I will say no, and you know I will use some kind of hand gesture, and because you know all of this already, I will do the last as indifferently as possible.

This only incites him. Still standing, he stops. Directly in front of the waggling girl.

Free ride, he tells her.

Northerly is pleasant looking but plainer than her patently beautiful friend, who is taller by a skull.

Free ride, he repeats.

She looks at him, then away at nothing and back again. Free?

Free, no charge.

She smiles uncertainly. This he understands to be a cue.

Really, no charge, he says. Come on, for you, free.

The string of words tricks out a flicker of accent. Two of them reveal an imported chivalry, sly and profligate. If he enjoyed a childhood sport, it was soccer.

She raises her eyebrows at Southerly, who does not react especially. He seizes on the pause.

On one condition, he says, slow enough to imply it was planned all along. If I make you laugh, I take you out to dinner.

He is comfortable with idiom. A foreigner, then, but not lately.

What?

Yes. If I make you laugh, even once, I buy you dinner. If you don't laugh, then no dinner. He holds her eyes, blinking only once his long lashes.

This time she does not look at her friend. She speaks their destination as a question, gets a nod and a second blink (a wink?), and settles into the pedicab. He watches, half turned in his seat. Her friend follows, pausing to look where she will place her ass before placing it. This, he has seen, is something only the self-regarding and the self-effacing do with their asses.

They move west, into the general orange of sunset. It is crosstown a number of avenues. The breeze is steady because his pace is steady. His path is not. Each time a car ahead goes recalcitrant, he veers toward one side, as if to complain to its fellows parked there, and just before he gives one of these a nice dent for not helping, he veers streetward again, pulling into a corridor not visible before. He makes co-workers of centimeters.

Perhaps Northerly wonders why his calves are not a bigger deal. Rather than protrude, they are simply solid, creditable without casting outward for credit, pistons in their sheaths. Perhaps she expects him to turn around so he can crack a joke, or make a face, or simply look back charmingly or impishly or goadingly or quizzically. He does none of these. In fact, as he pedals, he spends much of his time looking about at sky and storefronts as if he were on holiday, the pedicab a hatbox.

He slows. They have arrived. The girls step onto the sidewalk. Still he does not look at them. Northerly comes around to face him.

You didn't make me laugh, she says.

Make you laugh? His mouth stays open. *You* were supposed to make *me* laugh.

What? You said—

Make me laugh or I buy you dinner. This is what I said. And look—he crosses his arms like a big baby, tucking hands into armpits—I don't even think about laughing.

She laughs.

Got you, he says, grinning broadly. He gives the sides of her shoulders a slow, deliberate, two-handed pat.

I want my money back, she says.

Now he laughs.

Got you, she says, waggling this time her head in vague caricature and giving his shoulders the same double pat. She fights down a smile as her hands out-bounce in a pantomime of recoil.

Write down your address. Pick you up tomorrow night, seven-thirty.

Steadily she takes from her purse a piece of paper and writes on it and gives it to him.

Dress comfortable, he says. Tomorrow you're driving.

She laughs. He pulls his machine toward him.

You laughed a second time, he says, getting on. Now it's dinner and breakfast.

You wish, she says, allowing herself a giggle. She grabs onto her friend and starts walking.

He pedals slowly. Standing. Backward. Now, forward. He is underway as he calls out.

I like bacon with my eggs.

They are moving exactly apart. For looking they use the air over their shoulders. They speak to each other but call to the city.

What about names with your addresses?

Slow down, beautiful—he speeds up—Let's take this slow.

HOW TO MAKE THE SQUIRRELS JEALOUS

When it's autumn and grim, the air like a clinic's, friends trusted and friends adored turn idiot. They spout nonsense about liking the four seasons. I've got news. The third season is pure crime. Look, leaves. Every time the air moves, the ground seethes. Was there ever better proof of conspiracy?

When it's autumn and everything grim, the sky sere and withholding, the world is a great jar of dead things. My son and his laptop are loose in it somewhere, serious with ventures. My wife's at the stores hunting fresh turkey, talking about never frozen, talking about the pound-per-person rule, but they don't sell two-pound turkeys. What else to do but sit on a porch and make the squirrels jealous? I eat a thing like they do, in speedy nibbles with my hands hectic. It's a double business, my teeth the white worms plying a turd and my hands the dirty flies hectoring it. But I'll eat a massive thing like a double cheeseburger, or a personal watermelon wedged into halves with a house key. Or a meatball sub because that was the special every Thursday at the sandwich shop my father ran in the center building of a B-grade office park. Every

Thursday my father saved for me a meatball sub. He stashed it from the willowy receptionist who stood at the back windows in Qiana polyester, smoking and gazing at the retention pond and declaiming in a high mastering tone things better for muttering—*He tells her I love you he has to but who does he call My love? who's the only one he calls My love?*—audibly enough to startle the other customers into hoping they were not the ones being addressed. He hoarded it from the mortgage brokers who proceeded chest-first as if every step broke a different finish-line tape and who demanded everywhere the specials because the specials in all of life's departments were their due. He hid it even from the potbellied doctor who grew shy tufts in his ears and spoke like a hippo with a toothache and kept a pious regimen for health's sake by ordering every morning a bagel because 1979 admired the carbohydrate like 1999 the opioid and 1959 the cigarette. The bagel doctor rewarded this daily forbearance by splurging on Thursdays and going with the special, but God help the good doctor if he showed after 2 p.m. because even chances that by then the only remaining sub knew sequestration for the proprietor's son.

What is love, after all, if not a length of fencing between the loved and the rest?

That sub would sleep the night in our home's refrigerator between the butter, moon-gouged and crumb-furred, and the juice. Only so many times a kid can eat a cold meatball sub without hating it. Not my fault, then, when I started giving away—in exchange for cafeteria spaghetti with sauce closer to sweat on a coloring face than proper blood—the sandwich my father made with his own hands and warded off the world from and brought home specially for me.

Just as well because who even remembers what side items he likes and doesn't like.

The squirrels stare at me with those nearsighted looks, at once piercing and wobbly, like a seventh grader who takes off his glasses during lunch to look less bad when Laura Weller's sitting at the next table, even though this means he can't really see her, which may be the real reason because how do you exist successfully around a person as perfect as that? Their little squirrel chests rise and fall so fast it's hard to tell whether it's their hearts in awe of my haul or their lungs in anticipation of snatching it away. We stare at each other for a time. Then every one of them, every single one, scampers up, up toward that ashen disdain of a sky, up a tree or porch post, bushy tail trailing in conspicuous departure like the potentate striding across the tarmac who waves behind him for the clutch of snapping cameras but looks grandly ahead. This is how the squirrels console themselves. You may have bigger food, they think, and a bigger mouth to eat it with, but you fat useless lump can you do this?

I throw Cheesy Bits to the squirrels. I'm not a monster. The squirrels like Cheesy Bits.

When it's autumn and nothing but grim, this is how I console myself. You may have a faster metabolism and grippier toes, I think, but what kind of life is that, conquering branches and scraps, nothing dry when it rains, and you've never seen Laura Weller eat the meatball sub your father made, which is like making a part of you a part of herself, or heard her say, "This is amazing. Really. Thank you." I know two things: I wish the bagel doctor hadn't died of a heart attack years later in his own exam room but he did. And if you're jealous you should be.

YET IN THY KEY FOOD SHINETH

Two years I was at Scottleigh's Key Food. Register and restocking the olive bar. Olive bar was my realm.

There was the guy they called Mister. He lived on the bench outside Playa Bowls and showed off his phone, big-tap typing so everybody saw he had a phone, except it was a hand mirror. The high schoolers called him Mister Mister and sat on the bench and posted photos with him because high schoolers are asswipes.

Mister liked to come in the supermarket and pick things out and put them in his cart very careful. What he did not like was paying. When he got to Register, he'd just stand there, looking down, his hands on the cart. He wouldn't put anything on the belt. He wouldn't answer when you said, You going to pay for these? and then, You have to pay for these, and then, They going to make you leave if you don't pay for these, but he'd look up every time, which is why you thought he'd answer, but he never did, and he'd look down again as soon as you finished talking, and finally, after you realized you had to stop saying things or else he'd stay and keep looking up and watching your face, you did what he did, just stand there, and he'd turn and leave.

People said he was crazy. I say people are full of shit. Like paying is their favorite.

Hakim the day manager never let him near Register. They said Hakim got the job because he was married to the owner's daughter, and when she moved out, the daughter told her father to fire him, and Scottleigh said, You find somebody as good, I'll fire him. Scottleigh and the daughter didn't talk after that, is what they said. Hakim always spotted Mister on the way in or latest by Aisle 3. Mister was easy to spot because when he got to the end of an aisle, he pulled this thirty-three-point turn to haul himself around and went up the other side of the same aisle. Basically he was easy to catch because he was thorough. The only times Mister made it to Register, Hakim was out, and it was Laura on point, and Laura was busy talking grandkids.

That Christmastime, we were all getting in the spirit—Barbara from Deli put up decorations, there was a food-drive barrel near the exit, a Salvation Army was bell-ringing and singing carols like opera, and nobody knew if she was being funny or just trying hard—and the new stock boy spotted Mister coming in. I already saw Mister that morning, when I was walking from the bus. The high schoolers, extreme asswipes, now they were pretending to take photos with the hand mirror.

Laura was at Register, and the new stock boy gave her a heads-up, all whispery and side-eyed, like Her Majesty's Shitbird Service. Meanwhile Mister was doing his snake-with-a-sunstroke thing up and down the aisles. By the time he made it to organics, Hakim was at Register too.

Laura, seeing Hakim, started to say, I know. But Hakim put up a hand all serious. A few minutes later Mister brought his items to Register, and Laura scanned and bagged and told him a total.

Mister said, I don't have the money.

It was the first time any of us heard Mister speak. Maybe it was because the two of them there at Register looking at him. Then one of them because Laura just looked down.

Hakim just said: Merry Christmas.

Mister pushed his cart away. He was moving slow enough that the cart tugged and veered to the right every couple of feet. Almost out the door, he stopped. He lifted the two bags out of the cart. The new stock boy, who was like shadowing him, did a pro-wrestler thing with his shoulders like he was going to keep him from tossing the bags on the floor. But Mister ignored him. Mister turned the opposite way. Away from the stock boy, toward the wall. Toward the food-drive barrel. He set the bags down inside the barrel. Very careful.

Nobody said anything for a long time after he left.

Then the stock boy said, Well, shit.

Laura, bless her, she said, It's Christmas, watch your fucking mouth.

THE COCK CHIMBÍ

My uncle Omar knew the secret to killing flying insects. The key is fast action. The moment you hear a buzz, you slap the back of the shoulder beneath the offended ear with your same-side hand. "You kill it every time," he liked to say. "*Cien por ciento.*"

Tío also knew the secret to extracting a dog that's bitten down and won't release. Such a dog is one of three things: trained, rabid, or used to traveling in a pack. The trick is overcoming the impulse to pull away. Pulling away will only get you a deeper bite. Instead: you bend over, you grab the dog's hind legs, you straighten up again, you hold out your arms to full extension so the dog's jaws can't snatch at your belly or crotch, you shake him once like he's salt, you shake him a second time like he's pepper, and then you let go. As soon as he lands he will run like hell to find the food you were seasoning. (Not really. *Es chiste.* He'll run, but out of a freshly installed sense of helplessness.) Tío renamed people, giving them nicknames nobody else used. My father, Panagiotis, was *Pidi*. My sister, Marina, was *Marinuchi*. I was *Torito*. It means "little bull." Given Tío's illustrious dealings with the fauna realm—flying insects, biting dogs, fighting roosters—I considered it a promotion.

The Southeast North Tampa Facility for Wellness and Rehabilitation sits on Waters Avenue. The sign outside shows a snake-wrapped rod with palm fronds growing out of it. The fronds don't quite touch the caduceus. In modern graphic design, nothing touches anything. Things merely float near each other, suspended in a medium of wry suggestion.

I should visit Tío whenever I'm back in Tampa. My mother visits once or twice a week. She cuts his nails, combs his hair, grooms his nostrils with scissorettes. My sister sees him regularly too. When I'm in town, my mother's happy to go together. But I make it only every other trip. Maybe every three trips. I'm a third of a nephew, is the math on that.

My mother parks, and we use the side entrance. There's a keypad to the right of the glass door. We duck and shift to find the display through the sun's whitewash. My mother types in the code. The hackers of the world will one day realize they just need the grandchildren's birthdates.

There is no front desk. There is a central desk at the hub of three spoke-like corridors. We wave hello. The two behind the central desk wear scrubs. They may or may not be nurses. Everybody here wears scrubs. Most of them have oblique, process-minded titles like specialist, technician, assistant. This is a Facility. They facilitate.

The facilitators wave back. I should not be struck by their cheer. They know my mother from her visits. Also this is Tampa, not New York, and everybody smiles. Still. This unexpected warmth makes me want to wave a second time, or give them stock tips if I had any.

The color scheme is white, accents of orange and aqua. Thus does the corporate ownership give itself away. Aqua is Miami's color, not Tampa's. Tampa uses orange, sure, but for contrast depends traditionally on the only hues that can't provide contrast: red and yellow. A local outfit would know well the area's signature tri-and-fail-color.

We get to Tío's room. The slot sign outside lists two names. The bottom one is Tío's. His bed's on the far side, near the window.

Room's dark. Blinds are down and television's on. Tío's in bed, awake. I give him a bed-hug. I grasp his arm, not his hand, so that as much of my arm meets his arm as possible, and I wrap my neck over the top of his head, like a Saint Bernard keeping a rescue warm.

"He don't talk," Tío says as my mother comes out of her own bed-hug. He points at the other bed. "He never talks."

The top of the slot sign said "M. Yamahara." This is Tío's new roommate. Each time I come, Tío has a new roommate. This one's in his late fifties. That runs young for a place like this. In eight months Tío has not heard the man speak.

"Mister sleeps most of the time," Tío says. "When he not sleeping, he looks and looks. Just staring."

I look over. The roommate's lying on his back, blanket to the chin, head propped above it. His eyes are closed.

"Do you know why he's in here?" I mumble discreetly.

"He sick."

Tío doesn't bother moderating his voice. It's deep like a V-8 engine and rumbles like first gear.

"What's wrong with him?"

"Well, he don't talk."

Tío's speaking English. Maybe he thinks he can provoke his roommate into speech. This intrusive third-person patter is just another rehabilitative service.

"Mister, he puts his head on his pillow and stares. Like Rasputin. *Así.*" Tío impersonates a trance, eyes wide and lost.

I don't know whether Tío is calling this gentleman Mister because he doesn't know his name, because the dismissive reference is part of the larger provocation regimen, or because he thinks the first initial on the slot sign stands for Mister.

"Why do you call him Mister?" I say.

"I don't think he watching television," Tío says. He's using an indoor voice if a hangar serviced by pneumatic forklifts is indoors. "The way he stares. More like thinking about things. Remembering, maybe. Look at him."

It's pointless to look at him when he's sleeping. I glance briefly.

This backfires. Mister's eyes are open. The surprise causes me to do a double take.

On the TV is a documentary about the Maginot Line. Out in the hallway a person passes nearly every minute. They keep the room doors open. Nobody looks inside.

"Tell us about Chimbí," I say.

"*Quién?*"

"CHIMBÍ," my mother says, using the unabashed volume the aged use easily with the more aged.

"Chimbí," my uncle rumbles, smiling wide.

The hardest my uncle remembers laughing was the day he and his brother—my other uncle, whom they call Minito, but I've never met him—took turns carrying a young rooster sixteen kilometers from Demetrio's house to their grandfather's farm. Why they were carrying a rooster from Demetrio's house, I don't know. My uncle doesn't say.

On their way to their grandfather's farm—about six kilometers into the sixteen—they heard a noise, and turned, and there it was: Demetrio's prize rooster, a monster of a fighter, highly trained. It had been following them from Demetrio's house. The uncles knew the rooster wanted the young cock. Likely it had seen the youngster out of its pen and deemed this a good day to finally destroy it. Now the big rooster's eyes flashed, and its chest bulked, and then— the air blurred. No rooster. Only a dark mass that surged like a storm. Straight for them. The uncles ran.

The uncles knew if the big rooster caught up, the young one would die, inevitably, one way or the other. The uncles also knew they don't really take flight, these roosters, because arguably more impressive than flying is speed-skimming the planet, resembling other ground-bound creatures but whipping along at incommensurate velocities and thus terrifying their prey into a state of helplessness.

The proposition bore out that day, in that the uncles, terrified, chose to scramble up a tree and settle among the higher branches with their ward and without options. Farther from danger and closer to the broiling sun: this is what higher branches mean in Cuba. Hours they spent there, trapped. The fighting rooster marched around the tree, savaged it with a peck here and there, clawed the ground now and then, and, the one time it looked up, stared at them while shitting a shit so shitty there was no mistake it was registering a judgment.

Finally, sundown. The light turned: gaudy, wistful, heartbroken. And then, sun down, the fighting rooster simply walked away.

The uncles climbed stiffly out of the tree and went the opposite direction. Ten kilometers later, they were made to kneel in the dirt until midnight for coming home so late. To be clear, my grandmother's punishment for staying out in the dark was staying out in the dark. She was an atheist when the rest of the country, still innocent of Communism, was going to confession.

The uncles, not much else to do, picked a name for the young rooster there on their knees.

After a time, the uncles' father (my grandfather Severino, who apparently didn't ask too many questions) gave Chimbí to his friend Almentero to train. The young rooster trained hard—as Tío tells the story, I picture a montage involving tiny treadmills, and chicken-wire jump ropes, and guanabanas plunged upright in mud and painted with menacing rooster faces, so please feel free to do the same—and finally Chimbí was matched against an older brawler of a bird. The fight was at the barn behind Paneque's house, on a Saturday, because it was on Saturdays that Paneque's wife visited her sister, and so on Saturdays Paneque was king.

Everything happened too fast. Chimbí's fight was the very first contest that morning, and as soon as the two birds were loosed, Chimbí suffered such vicious pecks that with each of them his whole body vaulted from one part of the floor onto another. Three times this happened. Each time, the bully rooster's owner suggested they stop the fight. Almentero insisted they keep going. When, finally, the older rooster was spent, Chimbí attacked. And attacked. He showed such relentless vigor—a kind of focused rabidity—that the owner of the old rooster, fearing real damage, pulled his rooster out of the ring.

"Rope-a-dope," I say.

"*Cómo?*" Tío says.

When he isn't talking, Tío's mouth tends to hang open. Based on the data—he is fat and congested and upbeat—one might speculate this is for easier breathing and easier laughing. His lips, however, never fully relax. They purse a little even as they sag, implying something between an encounter with novelty and blunt skepticism. When you tell him things, you want him very much to believe and appreciate them because the pursed mouth makes clear he is trying his level best to absorb what you're saying. If he to fails to comprehend, then, this can only be your own fault.

"Rope-a-dope," I say. "*Lo que hizo* Muhammad Ali *con boxeadores más grandes y fuertes.*"

Those lips, equivocal, are called to duty as Tío keeps talking. Sometimes I'm not sure he understands me at all. But even when he doesn't, he remembers everything. When I first learned the term "eidetic memory," I warmed to it like a friend of the family. It knew my uncle.

The contest over, Almentero suggested the young rooster was the better fighter. In response the old rooster's owner made the only excuse he had left. "I didn't know that little shit of a rooster could peck so fast." Arguments from state of mind: ever the last refuge of the soundly defeated.

Almentero entered Chimbí in professional fights. For the first four, Almentero cut his spurs and replaced them with metal ones. Chimbí killed all four of his opponents. After that, nobody wanted to match roosters against Chimbí.

Almentero then let Chimbí grow out his spurs—they were black, and black spurs were rare—and Chimbí was able to fight a fifth fight because nobody recognized him. During that fifth fight, Demetrio, in fact Chimbí's original owner, stared and stared at Chimbí.

"You know," he said absently to Severino while still staring, "that one there looks like my roosters. A lot." *Bastante*. Hitting the first T in *bastante* so hard he visibly spit.

When Chimbí killed the fifth the same way he'd killed the first four, his glory was complete. And his career was over. Because now everybody—everybody—knew the cock Chimbí.

Originally my family lived in Weehawken. Tío and his family lived in Tampa. When we flew down each December to visit, my sister and I wore T-shirts and shorts. Always. Even in downpours and cold snaps. This was dogged ritualism. We needed the costume that was sparseness of costume to mark the occasion. We needed to show off our skinny and sunless limbs, our botany-club-treasurer limbs, our limbs like dishwasher-melted straws glugged with milk. That way the limbs would know we were in Florida and finally act like it.

Four round-trip airfares matched or exceeded my parents' annual travel budget. We stayed in motels. Their locations were determined by price point. Their parking lots, therefore, were extended highway shoulders, and the rooms perched like bleachers for viewing the worst race in the world, the drivers insensible they were in competition and uniformly wandering off course to middle-manage inside office buildings and buy eggs.

Cost cutting also meant we didn't rent a car. If we needed a ride, we called Tío. I still remember his home number. I tried it yesterday for the do of it. Automated message—"We cannot complete your call as dialed"— followed by that sharp little three-chord cadence that promises, with dotted rhythm and minor key, an urgent dispatch from somewhere important but that in fact constitutes a mockery, as the only callers who hear it are those who have just attempted connection with something important to them and learned it doesn't matter anymore.

Tío would pick up. Minutes later, he would pick us up. So that we, too, could non-race.

Mostly he drove trucks. Late in life he tooled around in a small SUV. But in the early years, before we moved to Tampa ourselves, when we were still making annual trips from New Jersey, he owned a Cadillac.

The Coupe de Ville was long and broad and sumptuous. Its name didn't lie: two doors, and this was a key part of the luxury. The newly rich, wary and a little stunned, dispense their wealth in bitty, reluctant parts. The experienced rich, familiar, grab armfuls and fling it. The anciently rich, inured to trophyism and finding an opposite thrill in calculated paucity, dispense their wealth in mindful, choreographed parts. *Of course there could be more*, says the dollop-sized foie-gras brûlée at Jean-Georges, *there always could be more*, says the middle hole in the merely three-holed Zegna belt, *and hence the intrigue of less*. Only two doors. Where sixteen doors could fit. The car's flanks boasted the square footage of a studio apartment. But the CDV was pointedly not a try-hard exercise in double-rich provincialism. It was a careless revelry in triple-rich discernment. *Two doors oughtta do it.*

My uncle was, without a doubt, the most exotic person I've ever known well. You get to know people and—you know how it is—they turn into what they are. Bodies with needs and opinions and appointments. They lose the sensational. My uncle never lost the sensational.

The list isn't getting smaller. He has gout, high blood pressure, high cholesterol, glaucoma, blood in his stool, and borderline diabetes.

He has a wife. She stands five feet tall, all of it able-bodied. She left him here, in Tampa, in a rehab facility, and rented an apartment in Miami. Her name is the Spanish word for "clear." Clear she isn't. Her only expressions are a smile so bright and admirable you want her to like you and a scowl so extreme it's from the movies. Her words, all of them lacerating, are jokes. They are, except when they're not, without warning.
If he gets any worse, he'll die. If he gets any better, they'll kick him out. It's a rehab facility.

Were Tía ever to come to this place, she would have to stop at the central desk. She wouldn't know she didn't need to. And she'd need directions to the room. *Alla tú.*

"Was cockfighting illegal?"

"*Cómo, mijo?*"

"Rooster fighting. Was it against the law in Cuba, like it is in the U.S.?"

When Tío laughs, he sings a tone and holds it. No barbershop singers join in, so he resolves with a heh-heh and, if he's not finished laughing, starts over.

"Tell me," he says, "you know if Christianity was against the law in imperial Japan?"

I have no idea. I answer how New Yorkers answer when they have no idea.

"What part of imperial Japan?"

"How many shoes you have?" Tío asks.

"Shoes?"

"*Sí.*"

"Like, six, I guess."

"Six shoes?"

"Six pairs."

Tío falls deeper into the pillows behind him and looks dreamily at the wall.

"I remember what year things happened," he says, "by what shoes I was wearing."

He's losing his teeth. He's got persistent ingrown toenails. His body, shedding its top claws, clutches the bottom ones all the tighter. He hasn't moved without a wheelchair in five years.

But no skin conditions.

"Mani, your skin looks good," my mother says. Mani is short for *hermano*.

"I go outside every day. The courtyard."

The courtyard has the highest concentration of Cubans in their eighties outside a Havana cemetery. These are ultraviolet light's core constituency.

"After lunch?" I say.

"I don't even ask. They take me. They know. The sun needs me."

"You need the sun?" Mom says.

"I don't need anything," Tío says.

Cuba is one of a kind, Tío likes to say. He declaims on the subject of Cuba's breezes, at length, in a state of rapture. He recounts how they blow at the same speed, with the same delicate and diffused intensity, as a human breath. How their duration so consistently, so eerily, matches the time it takes for a person to turn fully around, pausing at each of the four directions, which accounts for how thoroughly, and famously, they rejuvenate.

This is how it always goes when Cuba's breezes come up in conversation. And what comes next is always the same too. He passes his hand a millimeter above his skin, pantomiming the graze of a welcome breeze, and he says every time—*every time*, without exception—"*El aaaaaaaire, asíííííííííí, deliciohhhhhhhhso*," elongating the vowels in a carnal singsong, shoulders hunched, lips pouting more than usual. It is a mild trauma, to witness this show of overwrought delight. He still looks like a big and capable builder of houses, but moons and moans like a celebrity aesthete. Breeze talk is the only time I am embarrassed for him.

He also likes to point out, more matter-of-factly, that Cuba is the only country in the world that lacks venomous pests. It has snakes, sure, and insects, plenty of both, but none poisonous. What that means, Tío instructs, is this: wherever you happen to be standing, you can lie down there and sleep the night. Cuba is the only place where you can simply drop to the ground, exactly where you are, and rest with utter and peaceful abandon.

Also what that means, according to Tío: just as the desert wants shade, and the forest yearns for something bright, a place of peace craves a little violence. This is why, when Tío was growing up in Oriente de Cuba, cockfights were memorable happenings. They carried away sense and judgment. This is also why, at cockfights in Cuba, they kept outside a kind of counter—sometimes a bona fide desk, sometimes just a board propped on two cinder-block piles—usually staffed by a boy, too young to feel himself entitled to observe the proceedings inside, at which all the men stopped and stowed their weapons, guns and knives and machetes, before filing in.

He was fat. I never knew him not fat. His particular fat was a comprehensive girth, an outsizing of the trunk in all directions. It wore like a cloak. What he actually wore was the sartorial opposite: a shirt barely buttoned. All else equal, mass intensifies, compounds. Tío's bulk was no exception. It made his mono-buttoned shirt cling all the tighter, puffed the split placket halves into a double bandolier.

Other people have skin like rind or hide or textile. His skin was oiled wood. It looked hewn from something perfect because it was dream pelt: utterly and impossibly one-colored.

He was a home construction guy. He knew carpentry, electricity, HVAC. At a certain stage of a project, he was vanned to the house to push it from intermediate to penultimate completion. Plumbing, he did not do. I heard him say this, more than once, in Spanish, and in Spanish the front-loading of the noun makes it as categorical-sounding as in English. *La plomería no la hago.* He said this in the same contradictory tone, at once musing and vehement, used by prisoners of war when recalling their captors. Also like a POW, he never explained.

When finally it came time for him to leave a place, he followed the same protocol every time—almost every time because the one exception. First, he would rap something several times with a single knuckle: the underside of the table he was sitting at, the arm of the chair he was sitting in, the wall against which he was leaning. Second, he would announce suddenly his departure, in a sing-song, with the statement, "Well, lemme see if I get home." He'd go home, in other words, but *getting* home was another matter entirely. There were no guarantees. Surprise sinkholes, flash hurricanes, machete bandits. Who knew? He didn't need to know, is what the resolute knuckle communicated. He'd risk it anyway.

A couple times a week, he'd come over to my parents' house for a Coke and a chat. If my sister wasn't home, he'd ask how she was. Nothing unusual, right? But this was: he'd await the answer like the answer was something special. Like she was something special. Like he apprehended clearly her significance to the universe. When I moved away to school, then to New York, my mother would tell me how often he asked about me, about how I was doing. I could see him inquiring the same way, chin forward, eyes bright, quiet a moment to mull the answer. These are things he did because he thought so well of people. He consistently thought better of them than they thought of themselves. Even rotten people he'd condemn with a kind of awed spite. Leonid Brezhnev, Michael Milken, the Walgreens pharmacist who instead of answering the question would turn the package around and hold it up and ask, while looking off at the other side of the store, "What does it say? What does it say?" Of any of these, Tío might remark something like "*Maldito puro.*" But he'd shake his head, and smile, and float his eyebrows, in a way that seemed an awful lot like, *You got to give it to the guy.*

Who will think well of us now that he's gone? Who will ask how we are and cherish the answer?

My family—mother, father, sister—still live in Tampa. Each November I fly down to visit. Thanksgiving. I have no particular objection to wearing T-shirts and shorts. I have no particular need, either.

Each time she visits Tío, my mother brings scratch-made chicken soup. Or else she picks up a breakfast sub at Mambo's. They do a raftwich there of Cuban bread with scrambled eggs, onions, peppers, three kinds of meat. She asks them to hold the meat.

She used to time her visits for the lunch hour. That way Tío could eat what she'd brought him. But he'd eat the cafeteria lunch anyway, then have the soup or sub for dessert.

So she started going in late morning. She figured he'd fill up on the food she'd brought. He did. Then, after time to digest, he'd roll to the cafeteria for second lunch.

Not bringing food is unthinkable. "*Esta sopa,*" he's said to her, "*levanta el muerto.*" Her newest strategy is realpolitik. Acknowledging he'll eat the cafeteria lunch no matter what, she gets there late enough in the afternoon that he'll at least space out the extra meal.

We arrive. In the slot sign is a new name. In the near bed, sleeping, is a pale being in a ski hat. Tío's also sleeping. No surprise. Unless it's early morning or lunchtime, he's sleeping. We can't be dismayed. We didn't leave early enough to earn dismay.

Snoring, moreover. Tío snores like a cartoon. A stentorian noise, ridiculous, handy for signaling passing ships and loosening snowpack.

There's movement outside the window. A worker in scrubs is going home. He's walking toward the parking lot, parallel to the length of Tío's corridor. He's in his late twenties. He strides easily in the sun. He's the picture of contented anticipation.

Over his right shoulder he carries a clothes hanger. It streams dry-cleaner plastic. On the hanger: no tuxedo, no slacks. It's a polo-style shirt. Soft collar, short sleeves. Three buttons. What leads a person to invest so much, so fondly, in a polo shirt? Is it Florida, chary of crease and ceremony? Is it youth, sure only good things await?

Tío snores like the hinges of a great chest. He interrupts with a swallowing reset, appears to stir, falls to snoring again.

They are like jokes. What do you call a boy who can signal ships but grows up on a farm? A boy who can foil avalanches but grows up in the Caribbean?

Technically it's not a cartoon snore in one respect. There's no whistle on the exhale. Tío never whistled. Not in his sleep, not while awake. He couldn't whistle, in fact.

My mother and I stroll to the library, the courtyard. The facilitator at the central desk wants to talk Thanksgiving menus.

By the time we're back, he's awake. Mom asks about his sleeping, his eating. Tío's too drowsy for real answers. "*Bien*, Mani," he replies each time. Mani is short for *hermana*.

"Tell us about Chimbí," I say finally.

Tío raises his head and turns it fully. Someone just called his raffle ticket.

"*Ay*," Tío says, "*el Chimbí.*"

Demetrio's tenant-farmer let Tío see the coop with the chicks being trained to fight. One chick stood apart from the others. When Isidro wasn't looking, Tío snatched it and stuffed it in his pocket. Tío then walked over to Demetrio's house—Demetrio was Tío's mother's youngest sister's husband—and ate breakfast with the family. Tío knew that while *pollos criollos* (untrained roosters) make noise, *pollos finos* (trained roosters) keep quiet. My uncle had cake and coffee, the brazen thief, while Demetrio told stories from the head of the table and the contraband snuggled in Tío's pocket as quiet as a ball of lint. *"Pensó ese pollito que era su mamá."*

It was summer. Like every summer, Tío, Minito, and my mother were living on their grandfather's farm. Tío carried the chick sixteen kilometers to the farm. That is, he stole the chick. He raised that chick as his own. He fed him corn every day. And once the rooster was full grown, he named it Chimbí.

Chimbí lived in a pen on the farm but rarely stayed there. Tío's mother—my *abuelita* Alicia, who lived to a hundred and stopped making roof repairs with her ten-foot utility ladder at ninety-eight—was keeping a few chickens. But these, apparently, could not satisfy Chimbí. Regularly Chimbí flapped out of the yard to visit chickens on surrounding farms. Whenever Tío wanted Chimbí to return home—at feeding time, for example—Tío would simply grab one of the chickens. This caused it to flutter and squawk, which in turn, within a minute, never more than a minute, caused Chimbí to appear suddenly like a warlock, dark and rippling, then land, transform to calm, and eye Tío with the replete superiority of the mighty.

If Tío released the chicken before Chimbí touched land, everything was fine. If Tío failed to release the chicken before Chimbí touched land, Chimbí would jump—as if the yard were a mattress and Chimbí were merely bouncing on it—and peck Tío right in the neck.

Tío's grandfather's neighbor Barrefango had a four-pound rooster. Barrefango, a bachelor with gray in his hair, very nice but terrible breath, wanted to play the mentor. He proposed that he and Tío put their roosters to fight to see how they fared. This in Cuba was called *toparlo*—a test fight. Chimbí weighed only a pound and three quarters.

"My rooster's only two pounds," Tío said, too proud for fractions.

"If he gets in trouble, you can lift him out," said Barrefango. "No problem."

They set the roosters down on a penned-in square of dirt. Ten seconds into the fight, the larger rooster pecked at Chimbí. Chimbí took off running.

"Come on," Tío said. "Let's stop. I'm lifting him out."

Barrefango, who knew cockfighting, didn't look up. "No, no. Let's see what happens."

For ten minutes Chimbí ran laps around the dirt patch. The larger rooster sometimes gave chase around the edge, sometimes contented itself with a spirited back-and-forthing at center. Ten minutes of these desultory exertions left the larger rooster winded. That's when Chimbí launched into action and attacked the larger rooster with a vengeance. It was the older neighbor who then shouted to Tío to grab Chimbí and lunged to scoop up his fat rooster. Chimbí clearly was what Cubans called a *gallo corredor*, a leaner specimen that uses superior athleticism to tempt opponents into pursuit, tire them out, and attack once they're exhausted.

"Rope-a-dope," I say.

"*Sí, claro*," Tío says. "Rope-a-dope, *como* Ali."

Severino had a friend who trained roosters, and Tío persuaded his father to send the trainer Chimbí. After training a few months, Chimbí debuted at the cockfighting arena in La Maya. And won. Four times. He not only won every match, not only killed every opponent, and not only did these things in his first competition. He did them while boasting black spurs, very rare among Cuban roosters. Chimbí made quite a stir.

He enjoyed a luminous career thereafter, winning pots of fifty and a hundred dollars. Because he won—and killed—so consistently, it got harder to persuade others to match their roosters. Finally, Severino opted to have Chimbí's black spurs removed and replaced so people wouldn't recognize him. Spurs were usually extracted by stabbing them into the end of a corncob and turning, turning, turning the cob. Doing this a good while on each of three consecutive days resulted in a spur falling off on the third day. Then spurs from another rooster could be inserted in that same spot. (Weirdly, this was a common operation in Tío's day. Nature in its mischief often gave the gentlest roosters the most impressive spurs, and the most vicious roosters no spurs at all.)

Chimbí fought one last time after his transplant. It was at La Maya, and the pot was five hundred dollars. Severino invited Demetrio along. Severino also found a willing opponent, a bright-yellow, four-pound rooster named Pato. Its real name was Mazorca Dorada, meaning Cob of Gold, or Golden Ear of Maize, or Golden Corncob, a difficult translation because the original name in Spanish was—like every rooster itself—an absurd contradiction, aspiring to majesty even as it fidgeted goofily and smelled of farm. Maybe for that reason, or because Mazorca Dorada was the only rooster on the circuit that presumed to have two names, everybody called it either Mazorca, skipping the aggrandizing modifier, or Pato, the name given by those who refused to pretend it didn't look like a duck. Pato and its owner were ignorant that their opponent was the great Chimbí.

Just as the fight began, Demetrio remarked to Severino how much Chimbí seemed to resemble Demetrio's own roosters. That's when Severino told Demetrio the truth, how two years earlier Omar had stolen Chimbí from Demetrio's coop. (In fact it had been a year and three quarters, but Severino, knowing old sins were more history than crime, was too savvy for fractions.)

A minute later, Demetrio, excited, shouted, "Go Chimbí, go!" Pato's owner was scandalized to hear this— he knew his rooster's opponent by name and reputation, if not by sight—but it was too late to stop the fight. For decades the circumstances of Demetrio's eruption were a subject of some healthy dispute. Demetrio swore he had forgotten himself in his excitement and shouted his prodigal rooster's name inadvertently. But many speculated this was Demetrio's secret revenge, that he figured they'd stop the fight once he revealed Chimbí's true identity.

Chimbí won. And Pato died. The spur that dealt the death blow stuck in that fat sun of a rooster. It wouldn't come out. When the body went limp it sucked the spur farther in and released masses of soft tissue against it, like mud around an upright guanabana. Two men worked the dead rooster around Chimbí's spur, like a corncob, and finally freed it.

Chimbí was put out to stud. Thereafter he was known as Fourth Spur. He'd lost three spurs already. The farmers joked he was always looking to lose a fourth one, the only one he was born with, inside every hen he met.

"Easy, Tío," I say. I love hearing dirty jokes in my mother's company like a dog loves an upside-down shake.

Tío had a calm and stalwart manner. His self-possession was the contentment that people immediately recognize as a lack of need to prove anything. When he was caught out—my father, who likes to prove a lot of things, loved to challenge and contradict him, loved to undermine him factually—he would stare wide and blank, and mash his lips together, and tip his head to the side, a caricature of embarrassment. This hurt to see. I love my father. I can't say I love this about my father.

Tío watched television incessantly. Nonfiction exclusively. Nature, science, geography. News sometimes. But news can be thin, trivial. He preferred his juice in concentrate. History: this was his nectar. Wars, parchments, plagues, whaling, monarchs, bank runs. He found it all captivating and remembered everything. It wasn't just his factual recall that was uncanny. It was his relationship to the information—because as he related a datum from seventeenth-century France, for example, or ancient Sumeria, he related it with the partisan affection of a firsthand participant. When Lindy Jaworski tells you how she pooped her pants at a wedding, or recounts what her cousin said to make her laugh so hard she pooped her pants at a wedding, she does it with the enthusiasm of a proprietor because she owns these facts, she was there, and she's serving you a portion because you'll like it. Same with Tío and the transoceanic journey aboard the balsa paepae raft captained by Thor what's-his-face in nineteen-whatever-the-fuck. He'd describe it for you, all of it, like he'd been there, smelling the wet canvas cooking under first sun, agitated to distraction by the compulsive muck-clearing noise coming from the back of the navigator's throat, aching for a dry bed.

Back when he owned a home, it didn't have a backyard. It had a makeshift orchard. The trees stood mostly in rows. The crop, on the other hand, was heterogeneity itself. If it took height and formed bark, it was welcome. One of the trees grew hot peppers. I asked Tío what kind of hot peppers. He said tree peppers. *Pimientos de árbol*. Yes, like you, I had more questions after this answer than before. The point, however, is that the tree pepper tree was his favorite tree. If you came to Tío's house, you'd be shown his orchard, and if you saw his orchard, you'd be shown the tree pepper tree, and if you saw the tree pepper tree, then you'd learn what stage of tree-pepper-tree pepper season it was. During peak of season, Tío would reach up and touch one of the peppers briefly and then touch your cheek with the same and unexpectedly warm fingertip. If it wasn't peak, he'd tell you the story instead, make you grateful you'd missed by just a matter of weeks or months the prospect of a persisting red mark on your face from the surface oils left behind by a glancing touch of a tree-pepper-tree pepper.

"It's like Mother Nature kissing you," I said to him once, as we came back into the house through the sliding glass door.

His wife, my aunt, overheard from the kitchen.

"Don't be nasty," she said.

Around my aunt, around my father, around everyone else who was a trial—which is to say, everyone—Tío always kept gentle, always assumed the best.

There is just one tooth left in his mouth. The left one at bottom center. It is enormous, a monument vouching for how large and vigorous the man once was. It is easily visible because Tío still juts his lower lip out and down, even poutier than before. It looks like a catchment, constantly deployed in the hope of collecting something. Attention, interaction, surprise, something new, anything new, a thing worth observation, a thing worth judging but insufficiently engaging for observation, love.

The last two not really, if we're being honest, because, respectively, beggars can't be choosers, and the end of life isn't a Disney film.

I push him in his wheelchair to the dining room. The facilitators do not abide the term "cafeteria." The smell of gravy reigns. The tables are round. The residents sit four to a table, as if the tables are squares. I push Tío to a table with three women.

There is Máris, a little old lady who has nothing wrong with her back but curls up in a hunch and wears round glasses and generally creates an urge in people to fund a live theater production so they can cast her in something as the gentlewoman of peerless wisdom and boundless appeal.

There is Christina, whom a stroke has left lying back in a large, recliner-type wheelchair. The wheelchair is itself lined with a black synthetic cushioning material, like the faux-leather interior of a luxury vehicle. She looks forty-seven, forty-eight. Her eyes are very dark. Her hair is mostly dark. It has graying parts, but the match between hair and eyes gives her the benefit of the doubt. Her skin is smooth. But she says now that she has a grandson, two years old, who visits her all the time. *All the time* means every other week. The dark hair and flawless skin prevent me from believing she is a grandmother. The stroke has masked her movements.

The stroke keeps us from seeing how she would move, and likely she would move like an older person, and so—perversely—the stroke is what keeps her young. Maybe it's the match between hair and synthetic wheelchair-cushion lining that gives her the benefit of the doubt.

There is Lucy. From somewhere more South than Florida. She's blond, witty, poised. "They always seat me, even without a reservation," she says, looking around. "I must be important." Bursting with sass and one-liners. Nobody in earshot is listening. She doesn't mind. "I can't eat all this. Olympic trials are in three weeks." She reminds me of Ann Richards, once governor of Texas. In place of a national nominating convention, she addresses a soft-solids cafet—dining room.

An attendant in her thirties, face shiny and forehead embroidered with damped-down hairs, arrives with a cart filled with covered plates. She takes one and sets it down in front of Máris. Another in front of Tío. No gravy at this meal. Apparently the odor is a heritage scent.

Tío's the only one eating.

Why is the Chimbí story different every time? Not why—how? He can't be making it up every time. The detail, the conviction, the look and tone of remembering. The sheer mental energy required otherwise.

On the other hand, he can't be remembering the story. He's never told the same one twice.

I ask my mother. She isn't much help.

"You know your uncle," she says, looking to flag the attendant for napkins. "He's a storyteller. He tells stories."

Through the dining room window I can see the west entrance sign. From here the palm fronds don't like palm fronds. They look like a cartoonist's action lines. The caduceus is screaming. Or exploding.

A champion rooster once went twelve matches undefeated before retiring. Twelve matches may not sound like a lot. In cockfighting, it is an Elizabethan reign. A cock straining for survival knows no constraint. It will lash itself whole against a threat, and the manic unpredictability of whirring beak and juking spur tends to upend expectations and randomize outcomes.

This champion rooster's name was Allatú. The name was a nominalization of *"alla tú,"* in turn a Spanish colloquialism literally meaning "there you" and an expression of disdain for another's conduct or circumstance while claiming indifference. It is delivered with markers of disinterest—tired eyes, a shrug, a flap of the hand—and, though technically untranslatable into English, definable by triangulation from various near-equivalents like "suit yourself" and "up to you" and "good luck with that" and "you make your bed" and "knock yourself out" and "you reap what you sow" and "nobody has a gun to your head" and "let me know how that all works out."

Allatú in retirement was of course bred for progeny. His rooster descendants resembled him in that they had, most of them, a hole in the middle of the base of the ruff, so that the perforated ruff approximated an arch. The youngest of his sons—at once more restrained than his siblings and more alert—was called Chimbí.

Chimbí was fierce. He chased the neighborhood dogs and he killed two snakes. Tío wanted him tested. Severino put him into a single round at a small local setup. Chimbí won. Allatú's owner, Don Caba, still unresolved about his youngest rooster gone missing, saw a resemblance and came to my uncle's grandfather's farm to examine Chimbí more closely—and especially to confirm if the rooster had a perforated ruff. Chimbí did not take kindly to a stranger's approach. He flew up backward and made to roost on Don Caba's head, causing the man to lean back, which apparently is what Chimbí wanted because then he bent forward quickly and penetrated a neat hole in Don Caba's larynx.

Don Caba began to flail very carefully. He put an arm out at a strange angle, held it there, then jerked a leg out to match. Eventually Severino understood this was Don Caba's way of struggling for air and put his finger on the hole, doorbell-style, figuring this would allow him to breathe. It did.

The next fight happened in a hexagonal shed with four walls and two open sides. Chimbí was set to fight a different rooster owned by Don Caba. Don Caba—unable to confirm the rooster was Chimbí, incensed about a theft that may or may not have been perpetrated, moreover indignant that he was prevented from confirming what he could not know surely happened—turpentined his rooster. (In and around Santiago, cheaters put turpentine in the rooster's mouth. Out by Altosongo, in the deep countryside, they put it up the bird's ass, a quick dab with a pinky, because supposedly it enters the bloodstream faster.) The rooster was fury in bird shape. Twelve minutes the bout lasted. Every time it seemed Chimbí was finally recovering, and perhaps even getting the upper hand, he'd go down. The addled rooster so brutalized Chimbí that a spectator looking at him could tell he was wounded, and in more than one place, but couldn't tell which of these wounds was the most grievous. Eight minutes in, Severino walked out of the shed in what appeared to be disgust. Instead of leaving, he marched up to the counter outside, asked for his weapon back, pointed at the biggest gun he saw when the counter boy asked which, and walked back in, madder than when he'd walked out.

Tío hadn't seen his father leave, but he noticed him return because now he was holding a strange gun, and now he was pointing that gun at the turpentined rooster. It was at that very moment when Chimbí rose as if from the dead, not so much dripping blood as dropping it, in gouts, and took flight and—this is the incredible part, but Tío swears it happened—found Don Caba in the crowd and flew up on his face, causing him to bend way back in a startled panic.

Whereupon Chimbí pecked through the man's throat exactly where he had pecked it before.

The hole never really closed up. For the rest of his life, whenever Don Caba sang or talked or even breathed, his punctured throat made a high fluting noise, a whistling. Chimbí dropped from that man's throat and lay there and finally died where he'd landed. It is no small consolation to my Tío that Chimbí in his last act on this earth engineered a way to whistle sweetest music, through another, for twelve more years.

There is a song they still sing about Chimbí. It involves singing and whistling. Usually it's performed by a woman singing and a man whistling. But occasionally you'll encounter the rare artist who can sing and whistle at the same time. Tío saw this three times in his life. Two of these prodigies were men and the third a dark-eyed woman, and for this woman he bought a bottle of wine, plus one for himself. In Cuba you might more ordinarily have had a little rum or maybe Budweisers. But with wine you could be said to be courting, and these two bottles of wine had the largest and gaudiest labels of any wine Tío had ever seen, which was on purpose. He drank the wine, and he slept with the dark-eyed woman, and two or three days later, off on his own again, he happened to try to whistle and for the first time in his life couldn't, maybe because he was too thirsty, and the following day he couldn't either, maybe because it'd been raining all morning and the damp air spoiled his lips, and he tried again the next day and the next, and every day thereafter.

Tío never whistled again. He doesn't say a woman stole his whistle because that sounds ridiculous, and moreover, he didn't try whistling until two or three days later, so technically he can't rule out intervening causes. But on the other hand, he can't help but think it's true, and when thinking it's true, he can't help but think of all the things they did with each other that involved putting the mouth in exactly the shape one needs to whistle loudly and sweetly and well.

Tío remembers only the last two lines of the song.

The sweetest air is breath still in the throat.
Only the heart that stays wounded bleeds love.

Three things sent his ambient enthusiasm spiking:
shows of force (when Britain retook the Falklands he
babbled about it for weeks), extreme wealth, and good
food. He liked food so much, these second and third
things were really the same. Watching him eat, you
couldn't help but like food more. He breathed through
his nose—subterranean river, stamp press, subterranean
river, stamp press—as if the mouth had been relieved of
poorer uses and consecrated for a higher purpose. He
chewed with the upper and lower halves of his whole
head, so that the chewing you had always known, a
municipal affair of the lower face, suddenly seemed like
nice apprentice work.

Whenever we sat down to a family dinner, he'd call
out, every time—*every time*, without exception—"*¡Al
ataque!*" We all found this amusing, the comparison of
feasting to battle, the recasting of *bistec* and *plátano*
and *frituras de bacalao* as mortal enemies. But I realize
now that is a superficial take, and another interpretation
better obtains. A man fascinated like nothing else by a
historical account of war likens a meal to battle because
he wants—and fully expects—to remember it forever.

When I think of graduations, I think of him. He
attended all of mine, my sister's too. And he definitely
stood out. He dressed up, and the resulting finesse
jarred against his usual look. (I've told you already how
he only ever fastened a single shirt button, wearing it
like a tiny brooch.) Moreover, graduations are Anglo
occasions—the finery of the language, the Elgar music—
and he was a hulking piece of *caribe*. The fancier the
clothes he put on, the slicker he slicked his hair. But he
sort of *was* graduation, more than anyone or anything
else. Graduations, after all, like most ceremonies, are
content-free bullshit. They make sense only when
understood as gestures. They are pretext for celebration

and encouragement, for otherwise incommunicable fondness. And these things were my uncle's bread and butter. If Henry Ford were alive today, he could wear clown paint and in-line skates, but at a car show, they'd still make way.

So substantial and so specific, Tío. Like migrations, or palisades. Imagine a giant and ancient wheel, turning steadfastly, perpetually, its haphazard points up-pricking into others' days and others' lives. Now imagine it gone.

How can a man of such particular, striking, and invariable customs simply disappear?

It was a Tuesday when he was moved to hospice, my sister told me. He had a DNR in place. My cousin, Tío's son, let her know. "Come see him," he said to her. "We don't know how much longer."

On Wednesday my sister and mother went to see him. He was sleeping, did not look good. My sister peered closer. The skin not like wood, maybe. The set of the face? How he was holding himself, even lying down.

Thursday night, things were looking up. My cousin reported Tío was talking, alert, asking questions.

Friday morning. "You'll want to come see him," my cousin said. "The doctor says he's declined."

"Declined what?" my sister asked. "Like, water?"

"You know. Declined a lot. Like, his condition."

My mother and sister went and found the room. The lights were on. He was sleeping on his back, his face tilted a little toward them, toward the door. Quiet. No beeping. In hospice there is no beeping. What they were listening to was the hush of inevitability.

They walked to him.

"He's sleeping," my mother said.

"Should we turn down the lights?" my sister said.

My mother fixed his sheet. The top edge on their side was folded under itself. It looked uncomfortable.

"It doesn't matter," my mother said.

She sat down in the only chair alongside the bed. My sister pulled a chair from the wall and put it next to my mother's.

As soon as my sister sat down, my mother stood up, seesaw-style. She took Tío's hand.

"Is his chest moving?" my mother asked.

"I saw him move a little."

"When?"

"When we walked in."

My mother touched his right arm.

"He's warm."

They looked at him, Mom standing, my sister sitting.

"Is he breathing?"

"He's warm, right?"

That's when she put her hand on his hand. Not his arm. His hand.

The nurse came running. She ran at a speed associated with beeping. Her face was plain, predisposed to being pleasant, but nothing unusual. The hair that framed her face, on the other hand: dark and thick. Marina told me later she remembered contemplating this hair: it was from picture books; it was maybe wasted here on the dying.

The nurse put the stethoscope on, chickened her neck forward three times before she got it on how she wanted, all that Hollywood hair, and listened. Here, where truly all they did was facilitate, they were called nurses.

"He's gone," she said. "I'm so sorry," she said.

A man came in. He looked like a shift supervisor. He wore his name badge on a lanyard. This gave him the appearance of a man on the move, the one always checking locked doors, running his hands over new marks on the wall to see if they were more than paint-thick. He started speaking, calmly, about nothing directly. The number of other things he must have needed to attend to, and yet he was here. This mere fact was the most comforting thing.

This man of parts various, of duties multiple, then said, "Can I offer a prayer?" So this was the chaplain. My mother and sister didn't say anything. The chaplain said something about celebrating life.

My mother called her other brother, Minito, in Cuba. "It's just the two of us now," he said.

A different nurse came in. She looked like a nurse, had the hair of mortals.

"May I arrange the body?" she said.

My mother and sister didn't know the answer. My sister used the time spent not responding to realize the chaplain had left without her seeing. The woman went to the other side of Tío's bed and reached her hands toward him and then stopped and offered by way of explanation that if you waited to arrange it, it only got more difficult later, and as she said this, she kept her hands open and stretching toward and hovering, exactly as if she were warming them over a fire. Drawing no objection, she proceeded.

She stretched out one leg and the other. She took the two pillows out from under the back of his head and set one on either side of it so his face pointed straight up. She folded his hands on his chest. The left hand fell back down. She folded them again, and the left hand fell back down, and this time she folded the left hand *under* the right hand, and again the left hand fell back down and now knocked the right hand off, too, and one last time she folded both hands, and when of course the left hand fell again, she pressed her lips together in amiable surrender and just left it there.

Our cousin came in. He didn't touch the body. He hugged my mother. He hugged my sister. He looked at his father. He put his arm around my mother. How do you mourn people you love deeply without touching them? Why would you need to touch people you love deeply to mourn them? There are no answers.

A chaplain and two nurses. We throw experts at death because there is no answer. None of them know that if you bend your elbows and flare them out to the sides, so that your upper arms and the dog you're holding make a holy sign, you're doing it wrong.

The cremation people were picking him up. But maybe tomorrow because now it was storming. Our cousin had bought a ticket to Cuba. He was going to bury the ashes at Cemeterio de Santa Ifigenia, in Santiago.

"Because of the nonvenomous thing, right?" I said when my sister told me.

"It's the cemetery where *Abuelita* and *Abuelito* are buried."

"Oh."

"Did you say venom? What venom?"

"Never mind."

And then. They walked out, the three of them, into the lobby, into the parking lot. There was nothing else to do. Except stand near a sign advertising snake dynamite. What were they supposed to do? Life is what? A constant series of failures to not leave. They left. They left him there. I know this, I know all of what happened at the end, only because my sister and then my mother told me. It seemed appropriate that the story of a man who I knew through stories should end the same way, as a story told to me.

The hardest he ever laughed, he said. But when had he laughed? In the tree, out of helplessness? On the walk home, from exquisite relief? On his knees, in defiance of discipline, knowing midnight was on his side?

Tío never said.

The last time I see him, it goes like this.

Chimbí was a young rooster. Severino took him to a fight.

Chimbí won the match. Severino won ten thousand dollars.

After that match, Severino didn't want Chimbí to fight anymore. He didn't want him to get hurt. Chimbí died anyway. He wasn't even two years old.

"Is dying at two years old normal?" I ask. "For a rooster?"

Tío doesn't look at me. He hasn't heard me. He licks his lips. His eyes settle, like he's been trying to remember something and has finally remembered it. Then he opens his mouth again, to resume the story. But then he says:

"I don't know."

He heard me.

"Why did Chimbí die?" I ask.

Tío licks his lips.

"Maybe Chimbí died because he wasn't fighting?" I say.

Even as I ask the question, I appreciate what mawkish crap it is. It doesn't feel right to ask a question like that without a fake tan and a Classics 4Ever compilation playing. I go again.

"Maybe he needed to fight to be happy and healthy?"

What good are questions if they don't tempt answers?

Tío looks up at me, then turns away and looks at other things. In the bigger world, this would mean the question isn't worth an answer. But there is no judgment on his face, no malice or impatience. It's the earnest look of a person with nothing to prove.

The table is lousy with gravied plates. The platters, attacked to the white bone, loiter in the middle.

"I thought they climbed a tree with the little rooster," my sister says.

"Right," my mother says, "and hid in the branches."

"Do you want to hear the story?" I say.

My kids and my sister's have scattered to the backyard. They've discovered they get harassed less for excessive use of electronic devices when they use them outdoors instead of indoors. They will reappear with alacrity the moment dessert is announced.

"Yeah," my sister says. "I just thought it wasn't in the right order."

"It's the story," I say. "It's the story he told."

"Okay," my sister says.

"All right," my mother says.

My father makes two little circles in the air with an up-pointed hand. This is how he imparts dismissive indifference.

"I know the order," I say. "I'll tell it in the order."

"No, I know," my sister says. "I just thought it was out of order."

My mother doesn't say anything. She's trying to stay out of it.

"It's the right order," I say. "The order he told it is the right order."

The story was never the same. The order was never the same. There was no order.

"Okay," my sister says.

"Great," my mother says.

My father settles back in his chair, ready to listen, trying not to look like he's ready to listen.

Then I tell about Chimbí.

ACKNOWLEDGMENTS

I'd like to thank the literary magazines that first published these stories, sometimes in slightly different forms:

Beloit Fiction Journal: "The Cock Chimbí."

cream city review: "The Son of Butt Trudd."

Epiphany: "For You, City, For You."

New Ohio Review: "The Sisters Jeppard."

The Normal School Online: "Mr. Ambrosio Is an Idiot."

Petrichor Audio Magazine: "For You, City, For You" (republication).

Punchnel's: "The Wonder of Light Rail" (republication).

Rosebud Magazine: "The Wonder of Light Rail."

Ruminate: "*Katingo* Carried 15,980 Tons and a Gentleman."

The Saturday Evening Post: "Grossness."

Southern Humanities Review: "Heedless of the Wind and Weather."

Western Humanities Review: "Mighty Seven."

West Trade Review: "Yet in Thy Key Food Shineth."

I'm also grateful to the editors at those magazines for putting these stories to the world, for nourishing me with their enthusiasm, and in many cases, for helping to make the work better: Mollie Boutell, Roderick Clark, Angela Corbett, Chris Fink, Nick Gilmore, Ken Harmon, Odette Heideman, Fajer Alexander Khansa, Maria Kuznetsova, Alex Mattingly, Joe Mayers, Loretta McCormick, Stephen Parrish, Dan Ryan, Joe Truscello, Dave Wanczyk, and Emily Woodworth.

Additional thanks to the sponsoring organizations, judges, and fellow nominees for the following literary prizes and awards:

"The Cock Chimbí" was a finalist for the 2021 Story Foundation Prize.

"How to Make the Squirrels Jealous" was a finalist for the 2019 Lascaux Prize in Flash Fiction.

"Mr. Ambrosio Is an Idiot" was a finalist for the 2022 Fractured Lit Flash Fiction Prize.

"*Katingo* Carried 15,980 Tons and a Gentleman" was a finalist for the 2021 William Van Dyke Short Story Prize.

Most of all, I thank Cathy Kane, whose patience and generosity are the stuff from which these stories are made, and whose endless joy and warmth are kind of the point.

GEORGE CHOUNDAS (KOON-duss) is a Cuban- and Greek-American, a former FBI agent, and an NEA Creative Writing Fellow. In addition to *I Think I'll Stay Here Forever* (winner of the Press 53 Award for Short Fiction), he has published a book of essays, *Until All You See Is Sky* (winner of the EastOver Prize for Nonfiction), and a book of stories, *The Making Sense of Things* (winner of the Ronald Sukenick Innovative Fiction Prize). He is a three-time Pushcart Prize nominee with work in over seventy-five publications, including *The Best Small Fictions*. His Greek great-grandfather, a fisherman, was murdered by pirates off Aegina. His Cuban great-grandfather, a lumberjack, was killed by a tree off perpendicular by several accelerating degrees.